PAPER BAGS

A NOVEL

TRISH McDONALD

PAPER BAGS

A Novel

Trish McDonald

Woodhall Press
Norwalk, CT

woodhall press

Woodhall Press, 81 Old Saugatuck Road, Norwalk, CT 06855

WoodhallPress.com

Cover design: Asha Hossain
Layout artist: Zoey Moyal

Library of Congress Cataloging-in-Publication Data available

ISBN 978-1-949116-75-5 (paper: alk paper)
ISBN 978-1-949116-76-2 (electronic)

First Edition

Distributed by Independent Publishers Group

(800) 888-4741

Printed in the United States of America

To 'Everyday People'

CONTENTS

PART III: THE HUGGER/DANCER

PROLOGUE

I keep my fears in a ledger, tucked away in a paper bag. My plan is to have someone burn these journals when I die—someone I can trust to torch them, not read them first. There are secrets I don't want anyone to know. I was hoping I would never feel compelled to share my notes, certainly not pulled to confide in anyone. Now, circumstances have intervened, backfired even, and I've committed to writing a story based on my journal entries.

I was told, write what you know—write about your passion. So, even though I'm reluctant to share, passion was mentioned, and I know a lot about passion.

The story is fiction while closely following my own life. Characters are composites with embellishments to protect the legacy of the living and the dead.

On the surface, this is a love story, but it's not any love I ever dreamed about. This is a story that requires curiosity about fears, a sense of wonder in exposing them, and the courage to blow them away.

My fears are based on what others think and their judgment of me. But in truth, what I fear the most is that courage skipped me and went straight from my mom to my daughter. Somewhere in the middle, I got left out. Without fortitude, I ended up with curiosity—the writer's kind—a mind searching for a world free of judgment and blame. In my search to find such a place—loving and safe—I'm bringing along my yellow Lab Q. She's in the backseat with the paper bags—a witness.

"I am fearless. I am bold," I repeat, trying to convince myself I am resolute. My fingers tremble as I try to strike the match, to destroy the journals. I stop when I hear a distant refrain—a voice, wavering but clear,

"My dearest—a story wants to be told. A love to be known. A secret to be set free."

PART I
Kat

CHAPTER 1
The Woman in the Full-Length Mirror

As he inserts the silicone cups into the fancy lace bra and glides the fabric up his legs, sliding the nylon to his thighs, I'm entranced. I can't look away. When he leans down to put on the ankle bracelet, I notice he's no longer paying any attention to me. It's as if I'm not even here. He's completely focused on her—his own girly reflection—the woman in the full-length mirror.

I want him to look at me the way he looks at her. I'm actually jealous—jealous of an image in the mirror. Is that possible? What if he only wants her, not me? She's the woman he wants to be.

In truth, she's kinda trashy: short skirts, stiletto heels, garish makeup. She looks like a teenage hooker—as if she's fourteen right now. Never able to wear girly clothes growing up, she missed living those crazy days of adolescence as a girl. She's making up for it now. Stuck in a time warp, she'll continue to dress inappropriately for her age. As much as I love her, I can still be judgmental.

There's no question, I'm fascinated. But one thing is clear, in order for me to be a part of this coupling, I'll have to be an observer, a curious voyeur, a storyteller. I can't fathom it any other way.

When I confide in my sister Liz, the therapist, she chides, "Kat, this is not perversion; hell, it's not even on the DSM. Let's call it a fetish. It's just dressing up in women's clothes. Who cares if he wears lace panties?"

There are no rules for how I'm about to live. No books for me to read. No manuals with instructions for this kind of loving. With no set boundaries, something miraculous happens: I'm liberated. My puritan upbringing, the iron panties, and the warnings about men's laps, morph into a place far away.

I will not be prim and proper making love to a man in frilly underwear. And, oh dear Lord, I'll finally feel safe. Safe to say what I feel, what I want, what I need. He is clearly more wounded than I am. He has shown me his soul. As unworthy as I am, he needs to turn into someone else to escape his shadows. I become the Alpha.

Pulled by my need to learn more, to understand, I journal. The writing keeps my curiosity centered. I focus on my craft and the story I tell myself.

It's Christmas. I'm looking forward to the tree, the eggnog, and the gifts. He wants to go shopping for a velvet dress. To say I'm uncomfortable as we both peruse the dress rack in this upscale boutique is an understatement. I'm sure people know we're some kind of weird couple. As it turns out, he's just a very attentive guy helping me pick out my Christmas frock.

When we get home, he adorns his body with the requisite undergarments. As we pull the dress over her head, it slides perfectly down her body. The only problem is it's too long. Turning up the hem on this gown is a cinch. Little do I know, this vision of being fitted for a gown for a prom, a dance, a party, is her lifelong fantasy. Imagine that, me fulfilling her dream. She gazes down and whispers, "I've dreamed of this day. Thank you for loving me this much."

I wipe away the tears. This is what love looks like. But this isn't a love I recognize. This was never the love of my dreams. It's all very confusing. My heart is overflowing with love for this beautiful woman, yet I have no model for this love. Is it immoral, perverted, downright unlawful?

Coming up from my knees where I've been pinning her hem, I see her countenance so bubbly with joy. As I turn away, I hum a few bars of "Silent Night" and pull on my own holiday gown. No one will ever see our beautiful dresses. We're a party of two: two lovers, two women, a man and a woman? When I look back, I see two people deeply in love. This is the only story worth telling.

CHAPTER 2
The Stalker

Journal Entry: August 8

    Another day of no call. What did I expect? He's a ramblin' man so it's all for the best. But the love was incredible, and I feel grateful for having had him in my life. My friends think I should run after him, but I don't think I could ever do something like that—it would be pushy, aggressive. I never confront anyone. I'm more of the wait-and-see type.

Journal Entry: August 9

    I'm taking my friends' advice—I'm going after what I want.

    I look for love in the strangest places. My search is a combination of a writer's curiosity and my need for love and safety. Tonight, I forsake one for the other. I'm a stalker. In the dark woods, under the pines with the ground fern crushed beneath the wheels of my car, I hide and wait—for his truck, for his beautiful face, for his warm, slow touch on my body. I lie in wait as a predator takes over my soul. My perfect veneer has cracked. All inhibitions gone, no pretense of respectability, I have nothing left to lose. If I leave right now before he gets here, I might have some dignity left.

I'm pulled by a powerful force, something I've dreamed about and tried to avoid my whole life. It entails a certain vulnerability, an openness, a child-like desire: I'm going to ask, even beg, someone to love me.

This afternoon, I loaded up the car and headed to Sal's camper to get at the truth. A two-hour drive, there's plenty of time for me to practice what I'm going to say when I see him. The trip is miserable with rain so hard I have to pull over a few times. I arrive at the campground and he's still at work. It's nine o'clock at night, pitch black, and the rain continues to pelt the windshield.

I've never confronted anyone in my life. I'm more of the come-what-may type, never asking for what I need. I pretty much accept whatever any-one throws my way. Just as I turn on the ignition, his lights come around the corner. I'm embarrassed and humiliated. I have no pride. No longer perfect, aloof, and distanced, I'm going to beg him to love me.

As his truck comes into view, my heart is beating so hard I'm afraid I might have a stroke. He comes to the car; my hands are shaking, and I can barely roll down the window.

In an attempt at humor and to keep myself from sounding needy, I blurt out, "I'm not stalking you."

This gets a chuckle and in response he asks, "What are you doing here?"

"I'm waiting to talk to you to find out why you don't want to see me anymore."

"Wait here," he warns, then he turns his back and walks into his camper.

I do as I'm told; I sit in my car and contemplate my options: the boy? Me? Love? Sanity? How far will I have to go to find love and feel safe? As I wait in the rain with my Lab and my paper bags, I remember how it all began—my descent into this certain kind of madness—love-inspired, unworthiness-fueled, unhingedness.

Love is a curious thing. After thirty-four years of marriage, I wasn't interested in love. I was in the process of getting divorced, darn happy to be single. Here I am, living in a spacious fifth wheel trailer I never dreamed I'd own, right on the Gulf of Mexico in the Florida Keys. Coveting a trailer might seem absurd when I had a house in the suburbs, but the camper was freedom to me. I would live in it by myself, just me and my dog Q. My husband would not accompany me. We would separate and later divorce.

There was no way I wanted to get involved again, and on a quiet night in November, down by the water, I'm startled by the sound of splashing. Wondering where the sound is coming from, I turn to see just a flash of a diver hitting the water after a perfect jackknife.

As we do each evening, Q and I are strolling along the seawall; tonight we seem to have company. The splash that accompanies the diver is a reverberation from my past. And I'm back in college, standing on the three-meter board, psyching myself up for the dive. The photographers are lined up below, ready to get the cover shot for tomorrow's campus newspaper, *The Collegian*.

A competitive diver since I was a kid, aquatics was on the very short list of sports available to girls in the 1960s. While I loved swimming, I wasn't disciplined enough to spend the hours doing laps, so I opted for diving and continued on into college.

Back on the seawall, my curiosity aroused, I'm stunned to see what can only be described as Poseidon emerging from the ocean after a perfect swan dive into the sea. Now I wonder if this guy might have been a competitive diver too. He certainly has the form.

"What ya think, Q, shall we meet him?" My loyal companion looks up, gives me a wink, and together we head out to the pier for an intro.

His name is Sal, short for Salvatore, and he's adorable. Whatever is he doing here? The Florida Keys is where you go when you're running away, looking for someplace remote, determined to be a writer where Hemingway wrote. I start to babble on about diving, ancient history, and now I'm divulging too much information: divorced, trying to sell my house, and on and on.

He throws out, "You sound ambivalent."

Who me? Ambivalent? Couldn't be further from the…. Hmmm, got me. In thirty seconds, he has my essence: torn apart, at war with myself, creative yet tightly wound. Maybe he just got lucky.

I continue on undaunted, "Cookbook writer, nutritionist."

Softly he proffers, "Foodie."

In my best Groucho I counter, "We should cook together sometime." Turns out he's elusive, secretive, not available.

Ambivalence: Which door to choose? The door on the right says "Me." On the left, big and bold, is the word "Other." Choosing "Other" feels more like belonging, helping, not quite as selfish as the "Me" door. And here I am again, in front of this blasted door. I'm fifty-seven, and I'm being queried about feeling ambivalent. Is there some kind of sign stuck on my forehead and bored into my brain?

I was in the process of deciding whether to sell my house after getting divorced. Was I ambivalent about it? I was certainly unsure whether I had the courage to go through with it, but I never wavered about what I wanted: to be safe, to feel secure, to be able to take care of myself. Love never entered the picture. However, there were the stirrings of a longing for self-care, maybe glimmers of loving myself.

Ambivalence, the word that gets me here, as in the *Jerry Maguire* movie, "you had me at"— ambivalence. In minutes after meeting Sal, he has me pegged.

The very first question he asks, "Sounds like you might be feeling ambivalent, is that right?"

Great, I've just met this gorgeous guy and it turns out he's some kind of a shrink. Ambivalent, not me. That's a pretty big word with undertones that feel kind of dark. I've just made the biggest decision of my life, I've chosen to end my marriage, and this swan diver is getting a whiff of wishy-washy. Maybe Sal with his dark, curly hair and his olive skin is some kind of Italian wizard.

There's a shyness to him as he covers his mouth with the palm of his hand when he smiles. It's quite an endearing affectation. In fact, it's downright refreshing after all my years of being corrected and picked at for my imperfections. Here's someone who tries to cover up his smile, but there's no way to hide that twinkle in his eyes or the dimples in his cheeks. Plus, he might be some kind of a therapist, mental health background, or maybe he just likes words—a fellow wordsmith.

One thing is crystal clear—he's an empathetic listener. He had me with just one word, ambivalent.

Ahhhh, the power of words to hook me. "You want to sell your house, but you haven't put it on the market. You're getting divorced but you haven't signed the papers." Now I've met Sal and matters that need to be taken care of will have a new urgency.

Q and I walk by his trailer every day, hoping for just a glimpse or a sign of encouragement. He works six or seven days a week on a dive boat so there's no free time to casually run into one another. I give up on looking for him or even just running into him in the RV park, and I go shopping with the girls in Key West.

On impulse, I ditch the women and head to The House of Intimacy where I purchase my first vibrator. My luck, there are three college boys right in front of the toys. I keep my hand over the side of my face to try to hide the wisps of white hair falling out from under my cap and in the process drop my giant sunglasses.

As my disguise unravels, I quickly grab two Jack Rabbits and head for the register. I pay cash. I don't want this store listed on my credit card bill.

The second rabbit is for my friend Dora Jane, whose husband is sick. When she opens my package on her birthday with her son looking on, she curses the day she ever met me. It's one of our great friendship stories, one we will giggle about in our rocking chairs one day.

Back from shopping, I grab Q's leash and take her to the dog park. I round the corner and sitting on a picnic table is Sal, the diver. I'm stunned.

Out of the blue he asks me if I want to go out—then, now?

"You betcha," I say.

"How much time do you need?" he asks.

"I can be ready in twenty minutes," I reply enthusiastically.

Then he asks a rather strange question. "Can you drive?"

So, it's a little weird but sure I can drive. I hurry and get a shower. I don't think anything about this odd request.

We go to a bar, get some snacks, and have a few beers. I'm driving so I only have a couple. He seems to be knocking them down pretty good. All the while we're talking, he's rubbing my shoulders. Sweat is pouring down my back and my heart is beating wildly. I could take him right here. Damn.

When the bill comes, he says, "I have a gift card I was going to use, but our bill is going to be quite a bit less than the value of the card. When you use a gift card here, you don't get money back. We'll need to come back again on another date and see if we can use it all up." How clever of Sal—he pays cash for our drinks tonight, but we would spend the entire winter trying to use up that gift card.

Back at my fifth wheel trailer, I invite him in to see my etchings—oh. I mean, the pride of any self-respecting RVer—a full-size washer and dryer. He's in awe of my appliances. Kissing me softly, he turns away and heads for the kitchen. Uh, that's the wrong room, son. Pulling out the doggy bags, he separates out the leftovers so we each have an equal share. You're kidding me right now? Then he kisses me again, whispers, "Later," and heads out into the night, leaving me and the Jack Rabbit to find a fitting conclusion to the evening.

It would take someone from outside to break down the wall around my heart. I would not have known how to start. Maybe it would come gradually, a brick at a time. When I protect my heart from pain, I'm leery of love. I weigh it, measure it, give it a dollar figure, try to figure out the return on investment. What do I get back? Prestige, legitimacy, a dance partner?

When I start to dream of a companion, I want only two things: a hugger and a dancer. My body yearns to be hugged, held, and tangoed. In my mind I see a chubby guy who can only be described as the best hugger in the world. No idea why I see chubby; maybe the protruding belly will somehow enfold me.

In the dancer, I'm more discerning: rhythm—he has to move to the beat. When I dance with someone who has no feel for the timing, no sense of the drummer's count, and pays no attention to his partner's longing to foxtrot, I start to fantasize a different kind of tango. We are still talking about dancing, right? Some might call it dancing; it turns out to be what I call rapture.

Sal becomes my hugger/dancer right here in the Keys. We find what can only be described as rapture when we're dancing. Sal and I are in his RV with the music on. His love of music and where it takes him is a sight to behold. He closes his eyes and he's whisked away somewhere, that place he loves, some dreamy spot, a world where he might find contentment. It's not on this earth, this place. I'm making a leap here, but together we find it dancing.

It's "Harvest Moon" by Neil Young; it's got an upbeat rhythm. Sal takes me in his arms and it's like we're one person. I match his every move, his every step, his pause. We melt together.

As the music stops, he whispers, "Did you feel that?"

Did I feel it? It was as close to heaven as I've ever come. "Oh, I felt it all right," I counter. Then there's that part of me that figures it was the beer. I've even had one and I rarely drink.

"Do you think it could have been the beer?" I ask.

His answer is definitive, "I've had a lot of beer in my day and there's been dancing with alcohol, but I never had any kind of beer that could make me feel like this."

I'll call it rapture, this thing we feel when we're dancing. I know the music takes him somewhere very special; when we dance, I get to go there too.

Because I'm ambivalent, I'm pulled in two different directions. I want to focus on me and self-care, but I'm feeling a tug toward another. When faced with the choice, I veer away from the "Me" door, and I choose the one that says "Other." I become enchanted, even obsessed. Q and I walk by his camper every day, hoping for just a glimpse. But he's elusive and I become a predator.

From the dining room table in my fifth-wheel trailer, I discover an opening between the rows of RVs where I can see just a sliver of his camper door from my side window. I sit and wait and hone my stalking instincts. I peep through this portal, hoping for a casual encounter when he emerges. At night I lurk in the shadows, watching for his truck to appear.

This preying skill comes in handy later when I fall in love with my hugger/dancer Sal and he decides we're through. As I'm sharpening my predatory skills, Sal is hitching up his wagon to move on. It takes some prodding by others to convince me to go after what I want, and so I vow, "Oh, it's not over," with not even an ounce of ambivalence in my voice.

CHAPTER 3
The Yellow Lab

Journal Entry: May 20

    I don't want to have any more dogs. My heart is broken after the death of our black Lab Bo. I wanted to call him Velvet because his fur was so soft, but the kids prevailed with Rambo, later shortened to Bo. We've always had Labs. Our first was a female named Babe—now she was a great dog. When the kids were small, they had allergies and we had to give our Babe away. A few years later, she was found by the side of the New York Thruway with our tags still attached to her collar. We got her back and she lived to be fourteen. There never seemed to be any allergies after that.

    Her story and the 250-mile trip back to us became a tale we told to anyone who would listen. Now when I open the newspaper barely months after losing Bo, the first section I go to is Classifieds. This morning when I go to Pets for Sale, there's already a circle around "Yellow Lab Puppies, eight weeks old, seven females…"

❖

My very first glimpse of the furry little ball who is destined to be with me on my journey comes as I spot golden Lab puppies frolicking in the grass when we pull into the farm. Of the seven in the litter, one stands out from the others by rolling in the mud at the edge of the pond. Clearly looking for attention, she darts toward us, spewing mud and dirty water in her wake. My husband tries to get out of her way, but I bend down, relishing every ounce of her energy. Before I can get my hands on her, she's whisked away by the owner, hosed down, and dried off with a hair dryer.

Right away I can see she's going to be a handful as she squirms and fights to get away from the grooming. Meanwhile my husband is not so enamored.

He says, "Let's pick one that isn't so active. Maybe that one over there taking a nap."

"No," I assert. "She's doing the choosing, not us. And she's decided we're it."

"Hello," I whisper as I take her in my arms. "I'm Kat. I think you look like a little princess who will grow up to be a beautiful queen. So, I'm going to call you Q, like the alphabet letter Q, short for Queen."

When my husband grabs for her, she burrows in closer to me and I hold on tightly.

He glares at me and says, "Don't be like that, Katherine."

My husband never calls me Kat.

When we get home, I introduce Q to her crate. I've never used anything like this before and we've had lots of dogs. But I've agreed to try it.

Now my husband says, "She is not coming up to our bedroom. Let her stay down in the kitchen."

I'm in bed when the whimpering starts and then the full-out keening.

"Do not go down and get her," he warns. "You'll spoil her. She is not coming up here to our bedroom."

I grab my pillow and blanket and start for the stairs. When I get down to the kitchen, Q is frantic. I put the blanket and pillow on the floor, lie down next to her, and reach my hand into the crate to soothe her. She starts licking my hand but she's not settling down. I know better than to take her out of the crate so I tell her this will have to be enough. Then I feel her heart start to slow down. She must be exhausted. I keep my hand on her chest and we snuggle as close as we can through the bars.

Maybe this will work. I don't like the cage. I want Q to be curled up next to me, but I mostly do what I'm told. I don't take her out of the crate. We curl up with the metal between us and we bond.

After a night on the floor, I start to wonder why we would keep a puppy sequestered all alone. What harm could a little puppy cause in the bedroom? But most of all, how could a little furry ball ever become a problem between two people?

Later when Q and I move to the single bedroom, I whisper, "I need to get away, Q, to be my own person."

Now when my husband goes by on his way to bed, he says in a loud voice, "You want to end it, let's go, right now."

This kind of talk scares me and it makes Q start to growl. I tell her, "Easy, girl, I'm not ready to leave yet, but I want to."

As we're lying here, me in the single bed and Q in a comfy cushion on the floor, my arm dangling down to caress her ears, I tell her the long-ago story when escaping my growing-up family was my only option. In truth, I tell Q my story because we both want the same thing—to be petted, hugged, and loved.

CHAPTER 4
The Blue Satin Quilt

<u>*Journal Entry: Seventh Grade*</u>

Today is my first day of junior high school. Last night I dreamed I got lost and couldn't find my locker. Every time I turned a corner I was back where I started. When I got up this morning, my PJs were still damp with sweat.

The school is huge and even though I'm only in the seventh grade, I'm in a school with eighteen-year-olds. There's only one school for everyone—junior high and high schoolers all together. I probably shouldn't be so afraid all the time because my big brother Jerry told me he'll keep an eye out for me. He's just a year older but he's not afraid of anything.

I'm twelve years old, in the locker room at school, and I'm shyly removing my skirt and quickly pulling on the ugly blue uniform before gym class. I try to dawdle, to pretend my laces are knotted, anything to forestall revealing the bruises on my thighs; those ugly reminders of my shame. It's my own fault. I'm sassy, mouthy, a bad daughter; not worthy of anyone's love. Left to display my wounds for all the girls to see, I hide in a corner. After class I shower with my towel wrapped tightly around me. The blue satin quilt on my bed has failed to protect me from the blows.

The quilt, a gift from my Grandma McNeil, was made of the most beautiful fabric I've ever seen—royal blue shiny satin, stitched in a circular pattern and filled with thick cotton. When I pull it up to my chin each night, I drift off to sleep enveloped in what feels like a fluffy cloud of safety.

My bedroom is in a direct line with the front steps of our huge house with the four large bedrooms, two bathrooms, and a big dining room. There are, in fact, two sets of steps leading upstairs, one off the living room and one off the kitchen. The steps off the kitchen are steep and rarely used; we call them the back steps and they're mostly a depository for our dirty clothes. We stand at the top and heave our underwear down the steps. The washing machine is strategically placed near the bottom of the stairs so all you have to do is reach over, grab clothes, and put them in the washer.

Our house sits at the base of a mountain on the last street in town—a small rural village in western New York. Most of the people in town work at the local manufacturing plant, which produces glass products. There are engineers and inventors employed by the plant. They live in a fancier part of town. My dad is a transportation specialist who tells the truckers the best routes to use to get the products to market—a job my mother disdains—something she harps on every day.

We're all downstairs in the kitchen of our big old house: Mom, Dad, my older brother Jerry, my younger brothers Joey and Eddie, my baby sister Liz, and me. My mother's favorite, Jerry, the oldest, has a burly physique, a no-nonsense approach to life, and seems somewhat detached from the goings-on in the kitchen tonight. My parents are bickering, a nightly occurrence. My mother is berating my father for another of his daily transgressions, and he's standing behind her making faces and mocking gestures, which my younger brothers find hilarious.

My younger brothers Joey and Eddie are as different in temperament as they are in looks. Joey is dark and intense with curly brown hair while Eddie is fair-haired and gentle in nature. Joey is two years my junior, Eddie two years behind Joey. They're a matched set—they do everything together. Tonight, they've joined in the mockery of my mother.

I hate this display of disrespect and say, "Dad, stop making fun of Mom behind her back, it's not funny, you're not funny. And you boys, stop laughing."

Then my dad tells me to keep quiet, but I don't stop.

My mother starts up on him again, "You could have been anything, but no, you have no gumption and you let everyone walk all over you."

Now I'm emboldened and join in with my mother. "All you do is make fun of Mom and I'm sick of it. You think you're so funny but you're stupid…"

And with that last word, he turns on me and comes after me. My mother tries to stop me by putting out her arm to slow me down, but I'm quick and dart up the back steps, careful not to slip on the discarded laundry. My father, choosing the front steps, is pulling off his belt as he races upstairs. I dive into my bed and pull up the blue satin quilt to cover me.

"No, Daddy, no! I'll be good, I promise I'll be good!"

Too late for me. He's already fully enraged with no sense whatever as to what he's doing or why. He tears at my blue comforter, trying to pull it away. Holding me down with his knee on my chest, he brings the belt down again and again, the leather striking my skin. I desperately hold the fabric as best I can, but I'm no match for him. This is my dad and he's completely insane.

I watch from somewhere above as the sweat pours off his face and drops onto the satin, staining it with his rage. I've done this, caused this. Driven him to this brutality. I can smell the fear coming off him as he struggles to gain some kind of control. I see all this as I leave my body;

nothing but a faint echo of my brother Jerry screaming at my father to stop the beating.

But there's another voice in the background—a female voice. She's warning my brothers they have this to look forward to if they don't behave. In the distance I hear the kids in the neighborhood playing kick the can. If the window's open, they can hear my screams. What will they think of me?

Then I let go of the terror, feel the welts start to burn and the swelling begin on my back and my thighs, and I curl up and go inside. When it's over, I sleep but there's no comfort for me. The black and blue and ugly yellow take some time to appear. They're a constant reminder of my shame.

The blue satin fabric cannot protect me from the whipping. I have bruises that last for weeks. My mother never stops it, never comforts me. She stands there and watches. I lose my voice, in my own house, in my bed, under the blue satin quilt.

I'm a year away from becoming a woman when I decide it's too dangerous to speak the truth. I keep quiet; I don't say what I think. I pretend and I'm fake. My dad mocks my mom and I look away; I won't confront him because I know what happens when I do. This conclusion I came to in my adolescence is a pattern I follow for years.

The connection I make between anger and the pain that follows taints every relationship in my life, from friends to lovers to bosses. When I lose my voice, I no longer speak up; I clam up; I go inside. In my childlike mind I choose perfection: the smile, the teeth my mother so often remarked on, and the compliments I get for my disposition. I look happy but underneath I know the truth—I'm not lovable the way I am. I can only get people to love me if I'm perfect.

There's no harmony in our household. My mother nags my father for his lack of initiative, and he mocks her behind her back. My brothers get a big kick out of our dad's behavior, but I hate it. I have three brothers so I'm in the minority. My sister Liz doesn't come along until I'm nine and my mom almost forty, so I have quite a few years of reacting to the jokes and the mockery. My mother seems somehow oblivious to the goings-on behind her back, or maybe she does see it out of the corner of her eye but refuses to react.

I can't imagine how she could know about it and keep quiet. My mother is not a keep-quiet kind of person. She's always ranting about some kind of inequity, conspiracy, harm done to her, disrespect for her brilliant husband, the list goes on and on. This focus on inequality comes in handy for us kids when we get in trouble. Our mother is the original "my kids are always right" parent.

Way ahead of her time, she rails against anyone who would say a word against her children. Don't forget, she's a teacher herself; she once taught household physics in Brookside, Pennsylvania, and she knows more than any of those teachers in that school we attend. Later, when she becomes a home ec teacher, she will have a completely different stance on parents having any say whatsoever about her classroom.

Pretense and phoniness become my companions. We all learn this pattern of make-believe in our family of origin. No one ever tells the truth because there are consequences to telling the truth. It isn't like there are any big secrets—just two worn-out parents who have so many children they don't know what to do—yes, a nursery rhyme. Is that the one where they "licked them all soundly and sent them to bed"? It was the 50s, everyone got lickings, it was no big deal. But what if you were twelve? Isn't that a little old for welts and bruises?

I desperately need to get away. Sure, escaping my chaotic house is in there, but I want the dream and The Boy—a lovely blond boy in my seventh-grade class who lives on a farm with beautiful green pastures, animals, and what I start to imagine as an "idyllic" family. I figure all I need to do is pack my clothes and walk over the mountain behind our house, eventually to freedom.

The upstairs back porch with the path to freedom is right off my brothers' bedroom. Easily accessed, this is the scene of many a late-night foray for the boys who feign sleep and slip out to do whatever boys do in a small town late at night.

It's Saturday night and as we're all sleeping, there's a loud knock at the door. My sister and I tiptoe to the top of the steps where we can hear better. When my mother opens the door, the police are there.

"Do you know where your sons are, Mrs. McNeil?" they ask.

Indignantly my mother answers, "Of course, they're upstairs sleeping in their beds."

"Actually," says the policeman, "they're downtown at the station. We caught them with a gang of boys drinking in the park. You need to come down and get them."

My mother screams at my father to get dressed and get my brothers. A discussion ensues as to whether they are better off left in jail. Cooler heads prevail and they're brought home. We are all on edge as to what will happen to them. Would they be beaten? Grounded? Shunned? As it turns out, they are sent to their beds and no one ever speaks of it again.

My sister and I get back in bed. I hold her and reassure her things will be fine. I close my eyes, my own body shaken by the conflict. I try to whisk myself away to the serene environment over the mountain—the farm with its wide-open fields and a loving, peaceful family and The Boy. I don't want tonight's drama to scare me off my plan to escape tomorrow. All I have to do is get through church, then I'll be free.

In the morning, I assemble my meager belongings, grab the suitcase from the attic stairwell, and look around to make sure I'm not seen. No one seems to notice my furtive glances or nervousness. My baby sister Liz, who tails me like a hawk, is probably hiding under one of the beds to avoid our mother's Sunday morning hysteria.

Liz is three and I've taken her under my wing, hoping to shield her from my mother's mania as we get ready for Mass: big Catholic family on Sunday morning.

I'll help Liz put on her best dress and she asks me, "Kat, can I wear the socks with the lacy tops?"

All my siblings call me Kat and it's Liz's very first word she ever utters. She's so easy to please and even the smallest token of love makes her face light up with joy. When I help her with her favorite socks, I finish off with a big hug. She thinks the hug is for her, but in truth I need the hug as much as she does.

This day is a biggie for my mother. She parades us all down the aisle— her brood: my brothers, my sister, and me, five innocent souls heading to the communion rail of guilt.

In the middle of the chaos is my mother in her hat and white gloves, screaming, "I'll go without you—I will not be late." And here I am, with only one shoe.

"You'll go looking like a beggar for everyone to see," chastises my mother.

I search everywhere for the lost shoe and end up wearing my old ones with the holes in the toes. In my frustration I even look on the back porch, the site of last night's family drama.

As we squeeze into the car, we're a ragtag bunch—the boys with their buzz cuts ala my father's clippers, my sister looking like an angel, and me in my dirty old shoes. This is clearly not what my mother envisions when she sees herself and her children walking into Mass on Sunday morning.

When we get home from church, I see my chance. I grab the suitcase, stuff it with some clothes, and head out through my brothers' bedroom and onto the back porch. I get down two steps and come face-to-face with my mother.

"What do you think you're doing with my suitcase?" she asks.

"I'm running away," I blubber.

"Oh, you can go," she asserts, "but you cannot take my suitcase." As she grabs for the luggage, she sneers, "Get yourself some paper bags, they're more the style of a beggar like you." Then she turns and walks off.

I stand there looking at the back of her dress as she walks down the back steps, the same path I saw as freedom. My face starts to crumple, my chin drops to my chest, I feel the tears well up, my cheeks get wet, and I realize I'm not going anywhere. I'm not worthy of a suitcase. My twelve-year-old self has been relegated to paper bags. She couldn't care less whether I leave or not. I'm not lovable; she could never love a beggar like me.

As I stand there on what should have been my first steps to freedom, I make a fateful decision: I will become what my mother wants; maybe then she'll love me and not want me to leave. In my mind, I sign a contract to be the perfect daughter. On this day, I decide to smile.

In seventh grade I want to impress my English teacher, so I decide I'm going to be a writer. My new book, "The Mystery of the Silver Key," is highly acclaimed. My teacher writes at the top of my novel, "You have the gift of words." His words are a lifeline I hold on to for my remaining years of high school. Around our house, my words are not seen as gifts, they're seen as back talk and sassiness. I used to call them truth-telling but that didn't work out well for me.

We don't tell the truth in my house; we pretend. "Fine," you say when asked how you are. "Things are great, just fine." I'll never forget my brother Joey's retort when someone would ask him how he was doing: "If I was any better," he would begin to declare, and I should have known right then he was not ok. Not even the slightest bit fine.

My mom wears a hat and white gloves in a small rural village where she's seen as uppity. She has five children, no money, a smart, laid-back husband with no "get up and go" as she would call it. Both of my parents are college-educated, love Adlai Stevenson, rarely socialize, and are raising their family in the best Irish tradition they know, the Catholic Church.

My writing career goes on hiatus as English classes start to move to diagramming sentences and other archaic studies. In the absence of the type of English classes I love, I gravitate to Latin. Now I thrive on words and their derivatives; my vocabulary soaring with *veritas*, *pluribus*, *novitas*, not to mention my Sunday morning Latin: *pater*, *pax*, *mater*, and *dominus vobiscum*. My brothers are learning Latin also, as altar boys.

My mother would proudly boast, "Those are my boys up there serving Father O'Riley." Later when the little Italian priest shows up, she is not quite so accommodating.

Ethnicity, for the kind of Irish my mother was, always trumped Catholicism. If you were Italian in her neighborhood, she looked down on you. It didn't matter if you were Catholic or not. The little Italian priest was seen as pushy, loud, crass; the kids loved him. He was young and brash and sometimes irreverent—perfect for teenagers who were forced to go to catechism classes.

Everyone hated those classes, but if you wanted to be confirmed in the Catholic faith, you were required to attend. On the plus side, it got you out at night and your mother never knew if you ditched it or not. My brothers never told on me and I returned the favor—although I did have a goody-goody persona. They were never sure when I might turn on them, 'fess up to my mother, as I'm trying for her kudos.

Kudos is a Greek word, but it became for me a highly sought-after recognition by my mother, when on rare occasions she would bestow one on me.

"Katherine, you seem to like English and do pretty well with Latin, maybe you should be tutoring other kids as a side business."

Ok, I'm calling it a kudos because "atta girls" are rare with my mother, as are I love you and hugs. Hugs—I was so desperate to be hugged and loved and…

With that suggestion by my mother, I begin my side hustle as a Latin tutor. My students include classmates who know how to flirt, make up their eyes, and get guys when they flip their beautiful long locks. They don't know squat about *veni*, *vidi*, *vici*. I learn more from them than they ever learn about Latin. They teach me about wild boys and how to snag them. My writing career will have to wait.

"The first thing men look at is your smile and your teeth," advises my mother. I practice having the perfect smile—the perfect daughter with the perfect smile and the perfect teeth. I smile to get The Boy; I smile to get the grades; I smile to get the friends. I smile to show I'm happy. But the black and blue colors expose a darker vein that runs through my adolescent being—a darkness that pulls me to wild boys, rebellion, lying, and outright delinquency.

When I'm fourteen, I have my first encounter with wild boys. I'm tagging along with my older brother, fondly called "Our Jerry" by my mother. A "gearhead" by nature, he loves cars and speed and can always be found at a garage with his head buried under the hood of an old jalopy. Born fourteen months apart, we're a tag team match growing up. And we both seem to have the curious gene—that sense of wonder and the pull of adventure. When I'm three years old, he boosts me up over the back fence and then scrambles up and over himself as we escape our mother and explore mysterious places that are forbidden.

Later in our teens, Jerry keeps guard over me, cautioning older boys to stay away. Little does he know, I'm drawn to those boys, encourage their glances, all the while smiling my perfect smile. It never occurs to me they're bad choices. One cold December night, Jerry lets me ride shotgun as three of his friends race across desolate roads in the Southern Tier.

I meet my first wild boy that night. His name is Bear. Everyone has a nickname: Clutch, Rip, Mouse. Bear has the classic James Dean look, cigarettes in the rolled-up sleeve, slicked-back hair, a convertible, and a dangerous, leering smile.

I'm fourteen, innocent, ripe. He's eighteen, worldly, rough around the edges. He's every mother's nightmare. I give him what he wants and in the bargain, I punish my mother for her sins against me.

All I think about are boys and love, but my thoughts are jumbled: On one hand, love and safety are all I want, but on the other, I'm not a truthful person—I lie, pretend, turn myself into anyone or anything they want me to be. I'll do anything to please.

But what do I want and why are my needs so elusive? Is the unworthiness so pervasive as to render me needless? Imagine the jackpot someone hits when they happen onto me. I'll turn myself inside out. Just a little love is all I ask. And, I'm willing to be a sinner. All is well until that little voice in my head starts to tell the truth: "You'll never be loved for you, he only wants you for the sex." So, I try harder.

Unworthiness is the lens I look through when I decide who I love. Maybe one day I'll love and be loved for who I am. When that love comes, I won't know it as love because it will look like nothing I've ever seen.

I decide it's not safe to tell the truth. In fact, it's downright dangerous. I stuff my shame and unworthiness in my paper bags and drag them along behind me. I never pack away my curiosity. I keep it close. It fuels me, urging me to explore the unknown, the bizarre and dangerous. Now I'm starting to wonder if my curious nature has deviant undertones.

CHAPTER 5
The DNA—Mom

Journal Entry: Recollections from My Mother

My mother's twenty-eight and my father thirty when they're married. It's the middle of World War II and my father has been in Okinawa. They meet on a blind date set up by my dad's aunt. My mother's a teacher in a small Pennsylvania town where my father's aunt lives. His aunt sets them up and invites them both to dinner. If my dad's mother had any inkling of this cupid interference, there would have been no introduction. My mother and her mother-in-law-to-be don't get along. But then, not a lot of people got along with my mother. She was outspoken, opinionated, and did not know her place in the 1940s.

My mother's strong character would be the backbone of our family. When you add in my dad's brilliance, sense of humor, and humility, the offspring of this coupling would be five individuals of unlimited potential. That's the "nature" part, the science, the DNA. Then there's the other part, the one all the controversy is about, the "which is more important" part —nature or nurture?

❖

According to 23andMe, the ancestry people, I'm eighty-six percent Irish. I should know about addictions and secrets; I come from a long line of addicts, it's my heritage. When my granddaughter is given an assignment in school to search out the family tree, she asks me to help. I don't know a lot, but I do know my mother's parents came over on a boat from Ireland. My dad's family was Irish although a little bit of Western European comes up in my genetic profile.

My mother never talked much about her parents, but in the few stories she told it was clear her father had a hair-trigger temper. Whether he was a drinker or not, one can only surmise. My maternal grandmother, from her face in the few pictures we have, looks fierce. She runs the show with an iron fist.

My gut says there wasn't a lot of crying or other emotions allowed in that house. My mother is a prime example of her upbringing: No crying is allowed. "Start that crying stuff and I'll really give you something to cry about," she'd warn. We were to suck it in and act like everything was fine.

So how fine was it for my mother when her own father left her mother for another woman, while my grandmother was sick and dying? People didn't divorce in those days. You stuck it out and you kept the secret. I never met my maternal grandmother, but I'll bet she was a corker. She raised my mother to be independent and strong. I can still see my mom, at eighty years old, pushing the lawn mower up the hill in front of our house.

She gave us those genes, the perseverance, the feistiness, the indomitable spirit, and the stamina. We would also get the mania, paranoia, and the addictions. No, my mother didn't drink. She was way too controlled to let anything like alcohol weaken her will. There is, however, a certain type of "ism" that is related to being so tightly wound. I would inherit such an "ism"; it's called perfectionism and it's crucial for keeping secrets.

Mom is a bully. Like most bullies, she's scared of everything. She gets out in front of her fears with pure bravado. "You won't see me cry," she brags.

Nobody cries in my family. In the 1950s, everyone fears polio. My mother's fears are anal: pinworms and constipation.

In the morning we take worm medicine and cod liver oil. At night, before bed, we line up, pull down our underwear, and bend over the bed so our mother can spread our cheeks and check for worms. If we haven't had a BM that day, she fills up the enema bag.

Our rear ends bursting, we're warned by our mother, "You hold it all in until the entire bag is empty." Only then, after voiding our bowels, are we released to kneel down, say our prayers, and drop into bed.

I figure this humiliation is normal, everyone is dehumanized like this. My brothers and I don't discuss it among ourselves and we certainly never discuss it outside our house. When you spread your cheeks as your mother shines a flashlight up your butt, it does something to your soul. No one ever refuses; we're babies. Joey is the first to balk; he's always the problem child. "No," he screams, his face red, his nostrils flaring. "You can't make me do it," he declares as his fingers tighten into fists.

I watch Joey from my squinty eyes and I'm curious how far he's going to take this with our mother. Will she back down? Then he turns and runs from the room, slams the door to the bedroom, jumps into bed, and starts rolling his head and singing. I'm thinking this show of power is pretty awesome, but none of us follow suit. We are terrified of our mother.

No one ever cries. We've all been warned about crying. I don't remember how many years these anal inspections would go on. I do know I was old enough to have stopped it, to have said no. But, I was too weak, too scared.

Much later, when I reach in the paper bag of my mother's fears, I see a woman raised by Irish immigrants—people who have good reasons to be fearful. In the American caste system in the early 1900s, the Irish had to struggle to pull themselves up from the bottom rung. They would fight Italians, Poles, and Jews, all striving for respectability.

Newly arrived in the United States, and determined to be successful, my ancestors would choose education and religious vocation as their path. The "calling" would fall on my mother's sister, later known as Sister Stella Marie. This divine inspiration would rob my mother of her beloved sister when she leaves home and enters the convent. In the process, the stage is set for my mother's lifelong love/hate relationship with the Catholic Church.

Because the church trafficked in fearmongering, my ancestors are continually fearful of burning in hell. Steeped in these beliefs and the accompanying rituals of Mass and the Sacraments that require confession of sins, there exists a feedback system that borders on tyranny. My Irish grandparents' fears of not being good enough, not seen as respectable, seen as less than others, will push them to seek legitimacy through the Catholic Church. This legacy of fearfulness will be handed down to my mother and will come to be the story of my own life.

We all keep secrets. My siblings and I save one another. As part of a big family, we survive by helping one another. Our Jerry takes care of me. Joey is a big brother to Eddie. At ten years old, I become a mother to Liz.

When I'm eleven, my mother goes back to work as a home ec teacher. With five children, the youngest only two, my mother brings in someone to care for Liz. Wonderful, loving people come into Liz's life and she's spared our mother's wrath in those formative years. When my mother comes home from work, she puts her arms on the kitchen table, drops her forehead to her hands and, before she can mutter "Hello," is fast asleep. I will never understand how someone can fall asleep at the kitchen table until I become a mother; then I'll get it.

Since I'm the first one home, the first female, I start the evening meal. Joining me daily is Dick Clark and *American Bandstand* at four o'clock direct from Philadelphia. I cook and dance at the same time. Along with every adolescent girl in America, I'm in love with the star dancer, Kenny Rossi. Sure, I like Bob, Justine, and Pat, but I'm fiercely jealous of Arlene, who seems to be very possessive of Kenny. Now I'm curious. Are they in love? Does he just pretend for TV?

As much as I fantasize about Kenny Rossi, what I really want is to dance with him. *Bandstand* teaches me to dance. When I go to school dances, all the girls dance Philly style with each other. The boys stand around. They don't dance. When the music turns slow, they venture out onto the floor. None of them can dance. All we have is our fantasies with great dancers like Kenny and Bobby. It will be forty-six more years before I meet and fall in love with a great dancer. Coincidentally, he'll hail from Philly.

With a working mother our house is completely out of control. The boys leave clutter everywhere, shoes, shirts, wet towels. I assume the role of housekeeper. Now I'm the cook and the maid. It's the least I can do for my mother, who comes home exhausted. I hate to see the house in such disarray. The kitchen counters are piled with papers, tools that were used but never put back, dishes, pans, food. There's so much clutter I can't find a space for my meal prep. Not only are the counters overflowing, but there's a milk machine taking up half the kitchen.

This is my mother's answer to her five thirsty children who can't get enough milk. She's tired of buying it at the store. Her solution is an appliance that holds twelve gallons, delivered by the milkman in a huge metal container. Now I do know not everyone in my neighborhood has a milk machine. The size of the metal can on the front porch is a dead giveaway. My mother likes the fact she has something no one else has; she wants to be different, to stand out. Now it may only be a refrigerator-like unit, but its uniqueness sets us apart.

Later, this dispenser is a draw to entice boys to come over to my house. I invite them over for milk and cookies. Without saying a word, I take a glass from the cupboard, place it under the nozzle, and bring forth an ice-cold glass of milk with a heady topping of foam. Mom thinks my smile gets me The Boys. I know it's her milk machine. And, they keep coming back for more.

My brother Jerry is Mom's favorite, her firstborn, named after her father, Gerald. My brother is Gerald Lucas, and Mom calls him "Our Jerry." I'm not sure how the "Our" part came about since there were no other Jerrys around that needed to be distinguished from one another. But you can be sure once we siblings heard the endearing "Our Jerry" from Mom, we never let it go.

There was a certain bond between Mom and Jerry. He was always ready to assist her in anything she needed from going up the mountain to saw down a Christmas tree, to chopping the heads off chickens in our basement. No matter what she asked, he always came through.

When Mom was in her seventies, Jerry bought her a 1965 Cadillac she had coveted her whole life—yep, the one with the big fins and the huge grill in the front. That grill saved Mom and Sister Stella when they wrapped the car around a tree on a desolate ice-slicked road in Pennsylvania. Mom was a fearless driver, took corners too wide, drove too fast, and with the fins and wide body of this beauty of a car, she was in way over her head.

Now you add in her sister, the nun, who when you got them in the car together, one said, "right," the other "left." Who knows what happened that night on the way home from Snowshoe, Pennsylvania. Maybe the nun said turn right here and my mother did whatever she wanted and went left. The miracle is they were found—alive. That huge car with the eight-cylinder engine saved their lives.

When we were growing up, my parents responded to our curiosity with Pig Latin. As if we can't figure out what "ig-pa atin-lay" means. We'd ask them questions, they'd say "Nunya" as in "none of your business." This is not the 90s where everyone shares all their dirty laundry on tv and social media. This is the 40s and 50s, the idyllic time we long for, the good old days, the era when rugs are lumpy and bumpy from having so much swept under them. I'm curious about everything. Why do we have to wear hats to church? Why can't I be an altar girl? Why can't I walk around downtown with my friends?

My girlfriends love to come to my house to pick me up. Mom meets them at the door with her famous line, "Now, girls, remember to wear your iron panties tonight and don't ever sit on a boy's lap." They think it's a riot. I'm mortified. No other mother talks like that to her daughter's friends. If I had been braver, I might have asked, "Mom, why do you say those things to my friends, it's embarrassing."

In my heart I knew the answer. My mom thinks someone should give girls the facts of life: Men want only one thing and you have to always be on your guard. Maybe the better question is, "Why did my mother believe the worst about men?"

I don't know my mother's history and I'm never curious enough to ask. Whether she would reveal herself is doubtful. She's twenty-eight when she meets and marries my father; they have four children in six years. We are six, five, three, and one year old. A college graduate living in rural New York, my mother never leaves the house without her hat and gloves. The hat and gloves are her trademark, her statement to the town—this is a refined woman, a lady of breeding.

My mother has too many children; enough love for maybe two. I luck out, I'm number two. I'm showered with beautiful clothes. My mother never even looks at the prices when we shop. I come home loaded down with bags, never curious enough to wonder what the real price I'm paying is. The clothes are not free. With the clothes comes an unwritten agreement. I will do what my mother wants. I will be a good girl. I will look like the daughter of a lady. When my days get wilder, the fancy dresses disappear. I get a taste for teenage love, and I can no longer be bought.

I have no sense that I'm attractive, no self-worth, no self-love. Yet there are flashes of conversations when we're going out as a family and my mother says, "Don't stand near me, I will look old and ugly next to you." Later when I unpack those paper bags full of emotion, I realize my mother is jealous of me. How does a jealous mother raise a daughter to have a strong sense of self-worth? She doesn't. She doesn't stop the beatings, she doesn't comfort. Burdened with too many little hands grasping for her, she puts a wall around her heart. There will be no crying allowed; not enough love to go around.

My younger brothers know this. Joey, child number three, writes on the back of the picture of Our Jerry attached to my mother's bureau mirror, "You love him more than me." This raw display of pain is later used as torture and ridicule. It will come up repeatedly in our family gatherings with great hilarity. Here was the truth, never dealt with, which becomes the family joke. Remember the time Joey…

Eddie, child number four, is the loveliest of souls. He and Joey are a matched pair. They roll their heads and sing at night to fall asleep. In my house there's nothing strange about it. This is what people do to get to sleep. I whisk myself away to dreams of wild boys, they sing themselves to sleep. Our Jerry is at the top of the food chain. He does whatever he wants.

Years later my mother has Elizabeth Ann, known to us as Liz. She has it the worst. The rest of us have each other, which is how we survive. Liz has no one. We all go off to college and leave Liz alone with Mom and Dad.

Growing up, Liz is a chubby child. Mom serves donuts, the plate holds only four, and says, "They're not for you, Liz, you're too fat." We want the donuts so badly we scoff them up, trying not to see the tears rolling down Liz's cheeks. This is how we deal with a chubby daughter, this beautiful angel of a girl who idolizes me, her big sister. We're roomies; we sleep together. I reassure her nightly she will be OK.

"Snuggle up close to me, Liz," I whisper. "I won't let anything happen to you. You are a beautiful, sweet child. Close your eyes and try to shut out all the noise. I love you," and I start to sing softly and begin to hum as her eyes become heavy.

But in truth, I can't protect her from our mother's wrath. I can't even protect myself under the blue satin quilt. Liz is a witness to the beatings. She is three years old. Imagine what she thinks as we each leave one by one.

CHAPTER 6
The DNA—Dad

Journal Entry: May 5

I don't remember the exact words I said that caused my dad to beat me. I'm pretty sure it was more about my attitude than what I said. Maybe none of the words mattered—it wasn't me he was angry with—it was his whole existence and my mother's continued haranguing. I just happened to be mouthy, sassy, and within arm's length.

Now I'm Irish on both sides so I get the double whammy. My dad's mother is Molly McNamara. His dad, Edward, brings some German to our ancestry, but this paltry fourteen percent of my genes can't possibly compete with the heritage of the motherland.

Growing up, I can see my dad likes to drink and party but there is no money in our house for booze. My mother clutches the purse strings tight. Dad's only opportunities are his part-time jobs at night when he does the books for the local establishments.

The only fight I ever witness between my parents is after my dad has come home from his night work. When he comes in the door, my sharp-eyed mother spots lipstick on his collar. She goes berserk. Screaming, yelling, throwing things, she accuses him of cheating on her. Innocent and confused, he starts to put his hands up to defend himself. He has no idea what she's talking about. Then she grabs his shirt and points to the evidence: cherry red splotches all across his shirt collar.

"That GD Ray Price, that SOB, he did this when he came up to shake hands and start to give me a hug. Get away from me, I warned him to get away. He's always trying to start trouble. He did this. And he meant for you to see it. Wait till I get my hands on him," yells my dad.

A chill comes through that room like a blizzard has just struck our kitchen. My mother whirls on her heels, grabs her hat, doesn't even stop to put on her white gloves—this job will not require gloves. In a flash she's out the door. Whatever happens when my mother gets her bare hands on Mr. Ray Price remains a secret to this day. I wouldn't have wanted to be in his shoes that night. My mother is a force to be reckoned with.

My dad is a player; a man who would spend five years at Temple University because he loved sports, especially basketball. He was the original red shirt freshman in the 30s. Dad was the precursor to the trend of staying in college more than four years in order to graduate. Later he would build his horseshoe pits behind the house as a way to keep his playing alive.

When the boys get older, Dad introduces them to the game of poker. My mother loves this game because she always knows where her boys are—at the dining room table playing penny ante. No more police knocking at the door in her house. Dad will sit at the head of the table dealing the cards and calling out the game, "seven-card stud, five-card stud, jacks are wild." Our house is the local poker parlor—a great place for kids to meet. It keeps them off the streets. I make chocolate chip cookies in the kitchen while they play in the next room. The cookies don't even get off the baking sheets before they're gobbled up.

My dad was a smart man. During World War II, the Navy sent him to Harvard to be a codebreaker. A gifted mathematician, he would spend his work life at unchallenging jobs and never even try to take the CPA test he would have aced. My mother never forgives him for not living up to his potential. "You could be anything," she would rant.

Dad wanted to be a writer. With a houseful of kids and no money, there was never time for his passion. When he was able to carve out a few minutes, he would hole up in his sanctuary—a desk adjacent to the downstairs bathroom—and write on an old Smith-Corona. If the door was closed, you put your ear to the wood and listened. Tap, tap, tap—use the upstairs bathroom and don't bother Dad.

Overshadowed by the aura that surrounded my mom's character, Dad was like a plant whose growth was stunted because it never got any sun. He was quiet, never spoke up to defend himself, worked in a job that was beneath his education, was not compensated for his worth, became passive-aggressive, and belittled my mother behind her back.

To his credit, Dad had a wry sense of humor, loved music, and played the violin. People loved my dad because of his gentle, kind nature. The fact that he could turn into a monster in an instant must have come from the daily frustrations of life, not being able to stand up to my mother, being constantly baited by her, not having self-worth, having too many children, not having money, and the topper: a mouthy, sassy, truth-telling daughter.

There is another theory—men coming home after the war at a time when little was known or discussed about things like PTSD. What do you do with those thoughts about killing and the horrors of war? Most men went back to their families as if they had just been gone overnight on a camping trip. My dad never talked about the war. It never occurred to me my dad was angry at someone else. I was the instigator. I provoked his insanity.

Because Dad worked day and night, he was rarely involved in everyday family life. I believe he preferred it that way. He did the books for the local tavern at night, which I'm sure included all the beer he could drink and possibly a few side poker games. Since he was bringing home money, there was not much resistance from my mother. She must have smelled the beer on his breath, but I have no recollection of any fights that ensued because of it. I was usually in bed and asleep by the time he came home. Mostly, Mom repeated a litany of Dad's sins, spoken with righteous indignation, on a daily basis.

Growing up with three brothers, I play with boys all the time. My dad always includes me when he's playing catch with my brothers. I overhear someone say to my dad, "Wow, your daughter throws a ball just like a boy." My chest puffs up immediately. That's what I want to hear—how much like a boy I am.

My mother sends me for haircuts to the barber whose shop is in the lobby of the local hotel. You can imagine how feminine I look after having my head shaved with clippers. I prefer this style to the other option—my father's clippers. He has my brothers sitting up on a high stool out behind the house, a towel wrapped around their shoulders, while he buzzes their hair.

"Sit still, stop squirming," he warns as he grabs their heads, squeezing so hard he makes red marks on their temples. My dad hates this job and is always in a foul mood when my mom starts harping,

"Get those clippers on those boys, they're starting to look like shaggy dogs."

It's an ugly scene: the boys with their eyes tightly pinched, Dad growling, the dull clippers pulling their hair, and my brothers, each one in turn, trying to sit still long enough for it to be over. When my dad is done, they all look like waifs who've just come out of the hills.

In some ways I'm a tomboy. I'll never be a girly girl; never high maintenance. On our way home from school, the boys chase the girls and they run and scream. I stop, put my hands on my hips, and dare anyone to come near me. One guy who is very aggressive comes close. I put up my dukes. The boys teach me how to fight. There's a lot of fighting among my brothers. Joey has a hot temper and flares in an instant. Eddie is slower to get the burn. Our Jerry is not to be messed with; Joey only makes that mistake once.

We all learn to play our parents against one another. Mom always says no. Dad is lenient, he acquiesces to whatever Mom wants. We tell Dad that Mom said it was ok. We lie. A lot. I meet boys I'm not allowed to see—Italian boys.

In the pecking order of cultures, someone has to be at the bottom of the caste. My Irish mother believes she's above the Italians on that ladder. Italians are forbidden as dates for Mrs. McNeil's daughter. I make up a story, a lie about where I'm going, and I keep it a secret. Not even my brothers know where I'm going. I meet him, Vinnie, the forbidden one, and he teaches me about foreplay—how it feels to be a woman—what desire is. He only teases me.

Somehow my mother finds out I've been lying. She and my father confront me and they're a united front. I will never see him again. It's forbidden. That doesn't stop me. I've been bitten by desire. But in truth I'm a good girl and I want to be obedient, so I break it off. It's heartbreaking. I'm heartbroken. I come in the house and I'm sobbing. Crying hysterically, I blurt out "I did it, I did it."

"What," my parents scream. "What did you do?" My dad can barely catch his breath, my mother is crazed.

It suddenly dawns on me they think I mean I did it—it—intercourse. No one uses that other word that starts with an F. Quickly I say, "I broke up with Vinnie just like you asked. I'm a good girl." They both fall onto the couch, completely done in. My mother revives enough to say, "I know you are a good girl. Now go to bed." I go to bed, but I remember how it feels to have sexual desire, and I dream of Italian boys.

CHAPTER 7
The Banishment

Journal Entry: College

By the time I was in college, I knew in my heart I was bad at the core. I picked out a good man, a man who valued family and was helping to care for his widowed mother and his two younger sisters. I wanted his goodness, to suck it up and take it into my own being—this handsome man who loved me and wanted to marry me. I wanted to take his strength and make it mine.

I was so worried I was a bad seed, not worthy of anyone's love, maybe some of him would rub off on me. I got him to love me and then I took what I wanted from him, all the while not committing and making plans to split. I knew I feared taking responsibility for my life, but I never imagined I could hurt someone the way I did. He never deserved it—his mistake was loving me. I choose people who have something I want—in some ways I prey on them—like a vampire.

❖

At seventeen I couldn't care less about going to college. What I want is The Boy, the dream, a loving family. My mother, however, is adamant: propagate and educate. I make a covenant with my mother—the only school to which I apply—my mother's alma mater, my aunt's nunnery.

I'm on a college campus where my mother and her female siblings have all matriculated—Our Mother of Mary College, run by the Pius nuns. When you're about to bring shame on your family, make sure it touches everyone including your beloved aunt, Sister Stella Marie, of the Pius Order, whose Mother House is part of the campus of my college and sits on a hill overlooking the school.

My aunt is never referred to as Stella or even Marie in our family, everyone calls her Sister. When friends stop by they ask me privately,

"Why don't you call her by her name? Your mom is her sister; they played together as kids. What was her name growing up?"

I figured these heathen friends must not have understood how the church works. Once you marry Christ, you change your name. It was pretty simple to me. Much later, the significance of the formal name for your own sister would reveal a family of Irish immigrants, striving for legitimacy. What better path than the Catholic Church and the convent.

Welcome to Buffalo, New York, the city of my birth, snowiest city in the world. Home now to this rebellious country girl who will not be strong enough to escape her mother's hold. Too weak to protest, I fill out the application and agree to the terms and conditions: no drinking, no parties, no boys, no pants. No pants? It's 1962; women are not permitted to wear slacks, jeans, or any semblance of menswear on this campus.

The Catholic women's college is comprised of two dorms, a student union, a gymnasium with a swimming pool, and various classroom buildings. The campus is small and easy to navigate; however, there are not enough rooms in the dorms for our incoming freshman class. We're parceled out to homes in the neighborhood where I meet my two housemates.

My roommate, Maggie, lets me know immediately she's only going to be here for one year as she's already made her vows to become a nun. My other housemate, Sharon, lives in a nearby town and just happens to have a brother who's a priest. To top off all this parochial schmoozing, I am in a house owned by a woman who is impressed by the relational piety of my goody-goody housemates.

Even though I can claim a nun in my family, I'm seen as somehow less than the others. The housemother eyes me suspiciously, criticizing even my bathroom routine, saying things like,

"You make too much noise in the bathtub sloshing around. Are you getting water on the floor up there?"

While my infractions are minor, she is clearly picking on me and I begin to realize it's going to be a long year.

It doesn't occur to me that my housemother can probably smell smoke on my clothes and has somehow linked cigarettes to aberrant behavior. On campus, smoking is not banned outright but is relegated to The Smoker, a small room where I meet my tribe. The smokers are rebels: girls like me who won't conform and will challenge authority. In four years, seven of us will be suspended. I'll be the first.

When I open my paper bags with curiosity, I get a glimpse of my gang. In an environment void of men, our behavior takes on certain male characteristics. In this parochial school, we're oppressed and our response is bawdiness, even lewdness. Our actions and expressions are those of inmates. Our behavior is outrageous, like we're trying to prove something.

Our ringleader has the mouth of a sailor, sings the real words to "Louie, Louie," recites Nantucket limericks, and tells stories that thrill and excite me. I've never been around this kind of irreverence. It feels bad and rebellious and my curiosity is piqued. I want to be a part, to belong.

When I choose my college major, I'm methodical. I follow what they call in math "the order of operations." My "order" is: 1. Home economics where I learn to make a man happy, cook, sew, and nurture and 2. The MRS. Degree—the unwritten part of our syllabus that pretty much guarantees a mate. Note, however, that the loving family is not necessarily part of that guarantee.

My junior year I enter the Practice House, a requirement for a degree in home ec. This is where a woman hones her "get a man" skills. Eight of us will live together for six weeks, planning meals, cooking, and entertaining. We divide up the jobs including laundry so it's a lot to add on to your regular schedule of classes.

The house is a huge brick colonial with eight bedrooms, four bathrooms, a large living room, and a spacious dining room. The kitchen isn't fancy but has everything you need to cook and entertain. Most of the cleaning jobs are done on Saturday so we have a full week, not much time left for socializing. Today we are told one of the girls has invited her boyfriend to dinner. As we assemble to plan the party, the head nun begins to show us how to set up the table when we entertain a guest.

I'm way ahead of her, having already set the chairs around. I have, however, made a glaring mistake. I have not chosen the correct chair for our male guest. He must have the captain's chair, the one with two arms.

I balk. And just as I had done with my father, I start to object, with an attitude, saying, "This is so stupid. Who cares what kind of chair you…"

Sister Germaine, supervisor of the house, turns on me and raises her fist, yelling, "I've had enough of you and your mouth!"

Dear God, I'm about to be thrashed by a nun. Drawing on the power of the holy spirit and even Jesus, Mary, and Joseph, she stops herself before she beats me to death.

"Get out of my sight," she shouts as her spittle sprays across my face. This is one nun who will not be surprised by my banishment.

I am now shamed in the Practice House. In the paper bags with my shame is my jealousy of someone who would have the nerve to invite her boyfriend to dinner and we would all have to kowtow to them as a couple. She with her beautiful long hair, lovely clothes; she who brown-nosed Sister, and was a Goody Two-shoes. To complete my contrition, I will have to sit at that table, put on my all-purpose smile, all the while my hands searching for the arms of the armless chair.

Shunned by my fellow students, I gravitate to art, my minor area of study. Now I'm left-brained and logical but I have this piece of me at war. I don't see things the way others do. My right brain, the artist, struggles for just a glimpse of the light of day. I go to this place when I have nothing left. I make something beautiful out of this mess I'm in and I immerse myself in clay and linoleum blocks.

Printing thrills me the most because I never know what to expect when I stamp out the carved block. Because everything is reversed, my curiosity is aroused, and I can't wait to see the result. Black is positive, white is negative. Those places that are carved out on the block become the white, they call it relief printing. I like the word relief.

This art vocabulary soothes me. In printmaking there's no right or wrong. If I don't like the first print, I can work on the relief and stamp out something different with the next one. The concepts of positive and negative space and right and left brain thinking prove to be critical in my order of operations: 1. home economics degree and 2. marriage.

At the time I thought I was in love with the most gorgeous man I had ever seen. Dark hair, dark eyes, beautiful smile; he was a kind, gentle, loving soul. And he wore boots, working-man style, with mud caked on them. Tight jeans, boots, and a swagger and every woman in town turned to watch him saunter down the street.

He proposed to me, I declined. I wasn't worthy of such a good man. The fact that his mom had just passed away, and he needed a wife to be a mother to his two younger sisters was an integral part of the pact. Face it, I was just a kid myself; I wasn't mother material. I wasn't done with rebellion. His name was Jerry—the same as my older brother—Our Jerry.

We meet the summer of my sophomore year in college. He comes into the coffee shop where I waitress and he asks for ice cream. In my short, tight uniform I have to bend over the counter to scoop out the goodies. If I look up in the mirror at just the right time, I see his appreciative smile. Not a leer, just all-American gusto. We sell a lot of ice cream this summer.

My junior year in college, I invite Jerry to the prom. His job as a civil engineer sends him all over the state and he is worried about his sisters back home. The urgency in his voice regarding his home situation is a red flag for me and I sense where our conversations are going. He needs resolution and I'm the answer to his prayers. The fact I'm a home economics major gives me an edge.

The prom is to be held at Big Valley Lodge, a fancy ski resort south of the city. Enrolled in advanced sewing, I create my prom dress from a picture in a magazine. The dress has intricate layers of tulle sewn around the skirt, the top fashioned with a scoop neck and short sleeves. It's a lovely pale yellow and to complement the color, I weave a ring of purple violets and daisies in my hair. When Jerry walks in the door to pick me up, he's dressed in a white sport coat and in his hand is a wrist corsage of yellow orchids. My heart swells with pride that such a gorgeous man would choose me.

Funny how you can love someone in your hometown but bring him into your tribe and he just doesn't fit. He's come hundreds of miles to be with me on that special night, but I decide I'd rather be with my friends, they're much more fun than he is. He's acting like a prude, not joining in all the jokes and drinking games. As I push him away, he asks me to step outside and he starts up. "I don't like your friends, how they act, and I don't much like you when you're around them."

I'm stunned by his words, by his disdain for my tribe. How I ever thought this rowdy scene would fit into and enhance our love, I will never know.

Maybe unconsciously I did know. Maybe I knew it would turn him off and he would see me for what I was. Maybe I wanted a way out of the ready-made family, but I didn't have the guts to say it. Maybe I chose that night, with my friends around me in all their depravity, to put an end to us.

Now these are fighting words and I'm sensing a challenge and my rebelliousness clicks in. I've also been drinking so I'm fortified, and I retort, "No one is gonna tell me what to do or how to act. These are my friends and I'd rather be with them than you." When I realize what I've said, I try to backpedal, try to smooth things over. "Maybe you're right," I admit, "we should leave before things get completely out of control."

I decide to go along with ditching the party because that's what I do, I go along—but in my mind, we are over. Just like that—done.

Jerry has gone home and I'm still licking my Practice House wounds when my friends suggest we go to the Catholic men's school in town for something they call a mixer. It's here I meet Italian Wild Boy Tony, known as the baddest guy on campus. I get my first glimpse of him singing "My Girl" on stage. His hair is long and dark, and he looks disheveled. He's clearly on something. The crowd is going crazy for him as he gyrates and makes suggestive gestures. I'm fascinated by his outrageous behavior and I decide he's exactly what I need, an antidote to my Practice House fiasco and maybe a nice distraction from Jerry.

He asks me if I want to go out tomorrow night for a drink. "Sure," I say. I'm really curious how bad this guy is going to be. I love walking that thin line of danger, it gets my heart beating as I start to imagine our date. Will he have drugs? I've never even smoked dope so my anticipation is peak.

He picks me up at school and takes me to a local bar. He's been smoking pot and he's pretty mellow. We're both drinking beer but he's nothing like I expected—he's just a nice, gentle guy. It's kind of a letdown, nothing dangerous at all. He will, however, be my nemesis. Our one date does not end in the climax I desire—it ends with me and my alcohol breath coming face-to-face with Sister Gillian, the warden of the dormitory. When Tony drops me off back at the dorm, Sister is waiting for me at the front desk.

I've broken a school rule: no alcohol. I'm sequestered in a small foyer to await my punishment. In my panic I grab leaves off a plant and start shoving them in my mouth. Chlorophyll, right? My shame is complete when Sister Veritas, my English teacher, my writing mentor, is ushered in as a witness to my debauchery. I'm suspended, banished from my aunt's convent, from my mother's alma mater, from the grounds of legitimacy of the whole Irish family.

I'm ashamed to go home. My roommate, Jan, takes me to her house in Syracuse where we conjure up the story I tell my mother: a far-fetched tale of my innocence amidst the harsh rules of this old-fashioned, archaic institution. It's an easy sell. Turns out the pecking order in my mother's family has the nun at the top with the rest of the sisters and brothers a distant second.

In my mother's mind the nuns have an easy life, don't know what hard work is, and are out of touch with reality. Why would I want to go to a school like that? Good riddance! My relief is temporary. I can't make sense of the fact that I've just been kicked out of college, yet my mother thinks it's no big deal. I've shamed her entire family including her saintly sister.

As I unpack the feelings, I get a flash of the jealousy. My mother's sister has the easy life; a bride of Christ, she has legitimacy, honor, and a royal status. When we go out in public with Sister, we are treated like kings. Meals are free, we have preferential seating. The clothes she wears with her headpiece are called a habit.

"Make sure you wear your habit tonight, Sister, we're going out in public."

My mother's status is elevated in the company of her sister. How does that work out over time? My aunt would be shamed in the mother house because of my actions. My mother would find it amusing.

I was a bad seed. My mother's refusal to punish me created more angst for me than if I had been grounded for the entire summer.

When I come home after being suspended, I no longer want to see Jerry. I will break his heart. It's the cruelest, most life-saving thing I've ever done. When he calls, I tell my mother to tell him I'm not home. She hates doing it and asks me to reconsider. In truth, I think she likes him more than I do.

Now for some reason my mother decides I should marry Jerry. I have no idea why she would want that except maybe she figures we'll give her beautiful grandchildren. My mother's messages to me were always mixed: No, I should stay single, get a job, put off marriage, and in the same breath, maybe a home economics degree so I could teach just in case something ever happens to my husband. My brothers get only one direction: They are to be professionals—doctors, lawyers, pharmacists.

Mom turns all her energy toward who I should marry, and she tells me daily. Yes, his name is Jerry. Mom, you are so transparent.

"He wants a mother for his sisters," I whine. "I can't be a mother. I'm just a kid."

I'm tired of arguing. Banished from school, I need to get away. I tell Mom to tell Jerry I'm not home. Then I leave and she doesn't have to lie. I run away to parties and boys and summer fun.

This is also the season I prove my unworthiness by drinking, carousing, and escaping any touch with adulthood or maturity. I lie, cheat, and hurt others. Mostly I hurt myself. When I come home after being banished from the Catholic girls' college, I'm a mixture of shame, self-righteousness, and bravado. Steeped in years of pretending how nice I am, smiling and showing my perfect teeth, I throw back my shoulders and strut around like I'm some kind of queen. Emboldened by my mother's disdain for the whole parochial system, nuns, priests, even the Pope, I don a tiara of indignity.

How dare they discipline me? My boyfriend Jerry does not like my behavior; he doesn't like my wild college friends either. He thinks I need to grow up. I think he needs to get out of my life. This is all it takes to get my rebellious nature cranked up. Who does he think he is, my mother?

And so, I do what I always do in times of trouble: I run away from the conflict. Instead of confronting him and explaining my wounds, I flee to Canada, as far away as I can get. Well, actually it's just over the bridge from Buffalo but it does sound dramatic. A friend from high school, an old flame of my brother Jerry, gives me a hideaway where I can further my depravity. She has big male friends who are more than happy to oblige.

When I'm back home and I open my paper bags, I can see the disapproval in my boyfriend's eyes—he is ashamed of my behavior. But he doesn't know the real me. I never show him the faker, the brat, the bitch. He only knows the me I let him see, the one who wanted to catch the most beautiful man anyone in my town had ever seen.

Now I've caught him, landed him, made him fall in love with me, and I'm so immature I can't even be honest with him about how scared I am. How worried I am that I'm a bad seed, bad to the core. I can't abide that puppy-dog look in his eyes, that reflection of my own sadness, as if I've just peed on the carpet and he has to clean it up. I would just be another kid for him to raise, a burden added to his ready-made family.

As much as I want to be in love, I have to admit the passion just isn't there. Maybe what I love is the look of him, how handsome he is, his wonderful smile. Then there's the fact that other women gape open-mouthed when we walk by. I like the idea that someone that handsome likes me, but marriage, with a built-in family, two teenagers to raise—no, I don't think so. I'm going to break his heart and prove to myself and everyone just what a bad person I really am.

I'm out at a bar with my friends in my hometown when two older guys walk in. I recognize one as a basketball star from a few years ago but I don't think I know the other guy. My friends invite them over. I'm leery about why we would be hanging around these ancients. When introductions are made, I note the surname, a big Italian family in town. The talk is funny, flirtatious, with hints of intelligence and an undercurrent of sexual essences. Oh, I know how to do this.

The Italian is coming on to me and when he finds out I'm a home economics major, he becomes very interested. He has a history with a home economist but not someone who wants to marry him. The allure is someone who knows how to cook and take care of a man's every need.

Apparently, this other woman didn't realize when she chose her major that successful completion of the required courses included the MRS. Degree. But then maybe where she went to college, they didn't have the Practice House where it was drilled into you. Here I am juggling a marriage proposal from a good man and I'm flirting with someone else who already has his sights on me. Did I mention there was a certain incendiary smell in the air? I knew there were sparks flying around, but I also knew I was perfectly capable of spontaneous combustion all by myself.

Determined to prove how cruel I can be, I accept the Italian's offer to dance and I agree to a date, all the while knowing there is someone else. Someone who has popped the question; someone who thinks I'm special, who loves me deeply. Now who could love me, this paper bag girl, this bad seed? I cringe just thinking about how Jerry looks at me with those kind, loving eyes. He wants to love me, take care of me, heal me. I need to run away as quickly as I can. Italy might just work.

I'm wondering why I've never seen this guy around before, and he tells me he doesn't live here, he's just visiting his family here in this town. He's taking a course at St. Bonnie's for his master's degree, but he works in Syracuse, New York. He's a physical education teacher and he wants to become a director of athletics in the city.

When I tell him I just got kicked out of school, I don't pick up any signs he thinks I'm a loser, so I continue the banter. In the chatter I can see he is a planner with something to prove. He wants to set the world on fire, maybe my mom will like him. First, we have to overcome her dislike of Italians. Now that I'm older, been suspended from college, shattered all of her dreams by running away from Jerry, she might be a little more lenient about dating an Italian.

The next day when I tell my mom I met someone and a little about him, she already knows his entire life story. His father is not his biological father, no one knows who his father is. He's adopted, that means we know nothing about his family. Where did my mother get all this gossip? It's common knowledge in town, my mom sneers. Wow, this is going to be worse than I thought.

That night I get ready for my date with the Italian. I put on a lime green suit with an embroidered jacket and a tight pencil skirt with high heels. He doesn't even try to hide his pleasure when he sees me.

"Wow, you look fabulous," he declares as he comes in the house to pick me up. My mother concurs and demurely offers her hand. Who is this woman who is pretending to be my mother? What the heck is going on? Now I'm afraid my real mother is going to appear, so I usher him out the door quickly while my mom is still acting like some kind of countess.

We head to the only place in this town that can be called a night spot— the VFW. It's crowded and I'm on high alert. My eyes are darting around, and I look over my shoulder at the surrounding tables. No, if Jerry's here, he would be at the bar. But I don't see him. He lives in a different town so there's not much chance.... and then, oh God, I spot him at the bar.

"Come on, let's dance," I say to my date. I see Jerry start to head toward us; he raises his hand to get my attention. Can't he see I'm with someone? Unsure, he hesitates for a second and then he sees me as I wrap my arms around the Italian and start kissing him. Through my squinty eyes I see Jerry's heart break wide open. He stands transfixed, unable to move.

And with that level of cruelty, I crush someone who loves me. The worst part is I never tell him face-to-face. He finds out about my betrayal in a public display. When I look back into the paper bags, holding desperately to a sense of curiosity, I start to understand why I did such a hurtful thing: I cannot abide someone who could love me. I'm not lovable.

When my date gets up to go to the restroom, he leans over and cautions, "You're with me, don't dance with anyone else while I'm gone."

I nod my head. Got it. Rules, boundaries, conditions—just what I need. The timing is perfect. And best of all, my mother despises him.

"Too pushy, too much bravado, big talker, he's not right for you," my mother says. But mostly she warns, "We don't even know who his father is."

What? Like that matters. So, he's adopted, why does she harp so much on this?

"Maybe he's not Italian then," I say to my mother in my best smart-mouthed back talk. But my mother will be relentless with this refrain.

Now all my rebellious instincts are aroused—he's mysterious, family origin questionable, older, opinionated, established, and has a plan for his life. All he needs is a home economist. It won't hurt if she is at odds with her parents, banished from Catholic college, a little on the wild side—with an endearing reticence about speaking up or making decisions.

Eventually I have to face reality. My suspension is for one semester and I'm going to need more credits if I'm going to return and graduate with my class. Our Jerry is at Saint Jude College majoring in pharmacy. He takes care of everything: apartment, job, college admission. Our Jerry has connections. I'm to go to St. Jude for one semester and work as a caretaker for handicapped kids at The Home for Crippled Children—it's the 60s—that's the institution's name.

I will feed, bathe, and love these beautiful souls born with spina bifida, cerebral palsy, and other crippling diseases. All children, they instantly disarm me and break the chains around my heart. Now this is something of purpose. I feel more alive than I have ever felt. I could be happy here, giving love and receiving it back in barrels. However, my order of operations takes precedence. First, I will get my degree.

My St. Jude credits have been accepted and I'm allowed to return to the Catholic women's college to graduate. My Italian boyfriend picks me up at my apartment and we drive out in the midst of the 1966 storm of the century. Snow covers everything. Roads are closed. Somehow, we make it to our destination and as it is meant to be, he stands with me on the doorstep in Buffalo as I prostrate myself at the feet of the nuns. "Yes, Sister, I will be good. I promise."

When the nuns suggest he stay the night because of the horrendous conditions, he declines. I send him on his way, out into such insane weather I cannot even contemplate. I'm only concerned with myself; how I'll survive the next few months until graduation.

Are there enough paper bags to hold my shame? As it turns out, there are to be six more that night. I have company. The rest of my tribe arrive by train, stop at a local tavern on the way to campus, and are caught with alcohol on their breath as they walk into the dorm. They're all suspended.

We convene in the Smoker, all seven of us, trying to figure out what to do. Among the six is my roommate, Jan, who took me under her wing, brought me to her house in Syracuse not that long ago, after I was thrown out. The irony of this fiasco is not lost on me. Here we are, the second semester of our senior year, and what was supposed to have been my welcome home song becomes their banishment dirge. They've been told to pack up and leave before the rest of the students get here. They're going to graduate but they won't be able to take part in any celebration; their degrees will come in the mail.

Now, not only will I live the next five months in shame, I'll do it alone. I become an A student and lead a rebellion: a revolt against the matriarchy. A committee is formed, and we take our complaints to the president of the college. We will leave a legacy. We'll be remembered for our advocacy of women's rights—in 1966, women are allowed to wear pants on the campus of Our Mother of Mary College.

While I win that fight, the one with my mother continues. She comes to graduation and the party afterward. Turning to me with love in her eyes, she says, "You have the whole world at your feet. You're going to be something, make something of yourself, something great."

I've been waiting my whole life for these words from my mother—she's proud of me, thinks I'm destined for greatness. As I lean toward her for a possible loving gesture, she suddenly turns away, her face hardens, her lips form a thin line, and her eyes become small and intense. I'm wondering what has caught her attention and pulled her away from me. As I turn in the direction of her gaze, in walks the Italian.

CHAPTER 8
The Italian Husband

Journal Entry: July 4

I'm invited to an Independence Day celebration with my boyfriend's Italian family. It's a huge gathering with more food than I've ever seen in my life: interesting dishes like stuffed artichokes filled with meatballs, deep-fried zucchini flowers and fried bread dough that resembles donuts. And the showstopper—watermelon—carved up by the ninety-year-old patriarch.

Now this isn't just any watermelon slicing; this is a ritual where the paterfamilias stands elevated on the porch with the family gathered around and below. As the drama builds, the pieces of fruit fall away, leaving only the very center of the melon. The knife is poised in mid-air, drops down, and picks up the prized center piece as everyone holds their breath. Who will be the chosen?

I'm watching in awe of this powerful family tradition when someone grabs me and says, "It's you—Grandpa has chosen you!" I'm guided to the front of the porch as the head of the family points the morsel toward me. I gingerly take it in my lips and pull it off the knife. He leans down and kisses my forehead.

Now, when I catch my breath, I'm not sure whether I should bless myself or say, "Amen." One thing I do know is, I've been given a big Italian welcome into the family.

In my hurry to escape the brush with marriage and a ready-made family, I find my savior, the father of my children. In my paper bag with the shame and the bad seed is the feeling I'm not ok as I am. I'm unsure of my future, untethered, adrift. I'm also convinced I'm headed for trouble because of my rebellious nature, and I sense a looming disaster.

I'm not capable of taking care of myself as I've proven repeatedly in the past year. I glimpse an anchor, complete with a compass to keep me on the right course, a captain who steers the ship, someone who helps me stay on track, who's able to make corrections when needed.

I might need some coaxing in the marriage department, but I'm all in on rebelling against my mother. He helps me along by continually affirming I'm making the right choice by marrying him. My mother makes a mistake. She refuses to accept my choice for a husband. In doing so she pushes me into the arms of the Italian and seals our fate.

Graduation is over and I'm working a summer job as an arts and crafts teacher in my hometown. My mother thinks I should apply to teach here. I cringe; this can't be my life, in this small town—I'm going to need to get a teaching job, so I apply for a job in the big city—Syracuse, New York, where my Italian boyfriend works.

When I interview for the job in an inner-city high school, I lie about the reason I have no student teaching experience.

"I needed to work for a semester to help pay for my brothers' education," I explain. "So, I missed out on student teaching." Those words, a firm handshake, and my all-purpose smile get me the job.

A week later, I board the train in the morning bound for Buffalo, where I meet my Italian boyfriend, and the two of us travel together to Syracuse. Wearing my navy blue, double-breasted blazer with a scarf tied around my neck, I've chosen white pedal pushers for a cool, summery look. I'm excited and looking forward to finding an apartment, my new job, and a whole new life. This train trip seems romantic and adventurous and I start to flirt a little with happiness.

I've been successful getting a teaching job and I know my boyfriend is proud of me. As he exits to the bathroom, he lobs a box in my direction. All those years of playing catch in the backyard come in handy as I snag it. I open the box and look at the ring inside.

I sit there on the train, the box in my hand, my mind spinning. What just happened? Was that a proposal? I'm curious, is this a childhood prank—the way a preteen boy might ask you to dance—or, is this a twenty-eight-year-old man asking you to marry him?

When he comes back from the bathroom or wherever he's gone, he quips,

"I hope you like it; I bought the ring a while ago, but I wanted to wait and see if you got the job before I gave it to you."

Our engagement is predicated on my being gainfully employed.

This is where all my smiling practice comes in handy. And that step I took in the direction of happiness is halted in mid-air. Right from the very beginning it's evident, I will have to prove my worth. It never occurs to me to say,

"If you love me and want me to be your wife, this isn't the way you tell me or show me." But I don't say it; I don't say anything. I just smile and swallow the lump in my throat.

I doubt I have any romantic expectations; mostly I want to get away from my mother. I never fantasize a princess story with the ring in a dining car filled with cigarette smoke and the aroma of coffee brewing, everyone cheering him on as he places the ring on my finger; that isn't my life. I never even thought there would be knees involved or a meeting with my dad for the blessing. Mostly I was practical, methodical, measuring my responses, never putting my heart out there in the open. And I thought I was protecting myself by not showing my disappointments, not speaking up, not asking for what I needed.

My boyfriend has opinions, is self-assured and articulate, while I'm quiet, unsure and prone to rumination. Sometimes I rehearse what I want to say for days before I get up the nerve to speak the words. I've decided I want my own apartment until we're married. He thinks that's impractical since we'll be married in four months so I should move in with him.

Now I start my ruminating: My first job, my own place, I'm going to need space as I prepare for my classes. I'll tell him I need a spot for my sewing machine and all my notions, maybe a desk for all the wedding preparations. I practice how I'll say it for days before I utter one word. I'm nervous as I tell him, afraid he'll try to talk me out of it, but I'm fortified from all the days I practiced the speech in my head and I say, "I'm going to need to have my own place, even for just a few months…"

At first, he balks and starts to argue. Then he acquiesces and agrees to what I want. However, this pattern of rehearsing what I want to say will follow me for years and in all aspects of my life from career to relationships.

Even though I rarely say what I need, one thing is perfectly clear—we have a shared vision for our life together and he's determined to be successful. And a plan for his career becomes our life.

Had I been more curious at the time, I might have wondered why he was so driven, but by then I had already bought the ticket and the train had left the station. Sitting there, holding the box I so deftly snagged out of the air, I make the deal—I'll be the helpmate, the cheerleader— he'll be the star. Later, when his family asks about our betrothal, he says, "She was a great catch."

As I'm pulling up my wedding gown and adjusting my veil, my mother is in the background screaming at the top of her lungs,

"We don't know who his father is—this Italian. You can't do this. You will regret this. Mark my words!"

Now it's pretty hard not to "mark her words" when I'm trying to pull a gown over my head on the morning of my wedding.

My dress, a display model in the bridal shop, had been tried on a myriad of times by others but somehow must never have been quite right. Or maybe other brides wanted a gown that had been ordered just for them.

I love this gown as soon as I see it; it's perfect for me: a cape collar neckline covered in lace that falls across my shoulders, long sleeves, a full skirt of peau de soie, and best of all—fifty dollars. The fabric is luxurious as it slides over my arms and down my body, then billows out to encircle me. But it's the collar that says "elegant." I don't think I've ever seen another quite like it. The design and the intricacy of the fabric and lace is reminiscent of a dress from the Victorian era. I think my mom would have loved the gown if she could have let herself be happy for me. That's not to be. I'm all on my own, from the dress to the planning, rehearsal, and reception.

I ask my baby sister Liz, who's thirteen, to be in the bridal party and she's beyond happy. My mother stonewalls me at every turn, putting up roadblocks and even trying to negatively influence my aunts and uncles who are planning to attend. It's impossible for me to be happy in such an environment. Every time my lips would begin to edge up, my mother would give me that evil eye of hers and say something like,

"You're going to rue the day you decided to accept this proposal." Always ending with, "Mark my words!"

Last night at the rehearsal in the church and the dinner that followed, someone is glaringly missing—my mother. She threatened not to come but I figured she was grandstanding. My dad is here but then he's walking me down the aisle, so he was at the church earlier to practice. I look over at him and he's having a blast, on his second or third highball, no way he's going back for my mother.

My college roommate, Jan, is my maid of honor and she's appalled—you can't have a rehearsal dinner without the bride's mother, so she borrows a car and heads out to get my mother. It will take her some time to convince my mother she needs to be a part of this celebration. My mother doesn't want anything to do with what she considers a debacle. She has not been successful with threats or hurling her dire predictions regarding my decision of who I marry, so now she revolts and refuses to attend our rehearsal dinner.

I try to stall to give them time to get here. I figure if anyone can get my mother here it's Jan—she's been dealing with nuns and Catholic teachers since her days in prep school. Plus, we have the bond of both being suspended from the Catholic women's college, me first and then Jan with the other six of my tribe later.

I don't believe my mom will be able to resist Jan; after all, she has a career as a stewardess, and this impresses my mom—a woman who ran a restaurant in DC when she got out of college with her home ec degree. So, none of this marrying right out of college for my mom. Like Jan, she had a career.

I even got the same college degree as my mom. I was moldable, pliable, open to suggestion. The only dream I ever had was the desire to be a writer, which my mother instantly dismissed as impractical. Of course, she's had years of practice—telling my dad the same thing—

"You'll never get rich writing a book, you have a family to feed, bills to pay…"

At the rehearsal dinner, the staff is serving the meal when the door opens and in walks my mother, dressed like a queen with long white gloves I've never seen before. Perched on her head is a brand-new hat with a veil. If it had been white, the whole room would have gasped. My mother must have been sitting there just waiting for someone to get her. But then this is the kind of entrance my mother likes, and she takes her seat at my side. I bow my head ever so slightly, giving her her due.

"Good evening, Mother," I say. "Nice of you to join us." She turns her head away from me and starts on her salad.

The next morning the house is buzzing with activity. I get in the bathroom early because I know things are going to get dicey. Little do I know my mother has been rehearsing her diatribe all night. She doesn't care who hears her, she's adamant in her disappointment in me.

"We don't know who his father is," she screams. "We don't know who his family is—this Italian!"

And the longer this goes on, the surer I am I'm making the right decision. All I want to do is get out of here, out of her life, away from this shrew that won't stop screaming. All around me people are tiptoeing; no one wants to incur my mother's wrath. She's fully enraged and I'm the recipient. I never say a word. I know better and it wouldn't do any good anyway.

And so, I'm married in the Catholic Church to the Italian. Afterward we have a big reception with dinner, dancing, and all his family in attendance. I love his big Italian family—they are fun-loving, boisterous, and enjoying the food and celebratory atmosphere to the hilt. And they seem to like me a lot. Maybe they're relieved to have their son settling down and getting married to what seems to be a lovely, practical-minded woman with a great smile.

Things are going pretty well. My aunt Sister Stella has cornered my mother and is keeping us apart. After we cut the cake and it's time for us to leave the reception, we walk toward the door. My husband's stepfather is standing by the door, his cheeks wet with tears. He starts wiping his eyes with his handkerchief as we approach. Out of nowhere my mother appears, turns to him, and says,

"Don't think I'm going to shed any tears over her. This was her choice, she's the one who will be crying in the days to come."

Then off she storms, leaving a trail of smoke behind her. I turn to my stepfather-in-law and shrug my shoulders, saying,

"Don't pay any attention to her, she's a little dramatic." But I remember her words to this day.

Yes, I mark her words. Of course, she's prescient. My mother knows me. Mothers know what is best for their children. When rebellion takes over, there's no thinking, not for me anyway. With curiosity, I wonder if I would have come to a different conclusion if I hadn't been so determined to hurt my mother.

If she had said to me, "Katherine, I trust your judgment. I know you'll make the right decision about this marriage proposal."

That clearly won't happen; isn't even on the radar. My mother is terrified of losing me to this brash, bold Italian and so she pushes me away and into his arms. I'm so lost; in need of someone strong to hold on to. I grasp for his hand and he offers me everything I need: stability, direction, and most of all love and assurance that I'm doing the right thing.

"You're making the right decision by marrying me," he assures me. And I fall in love with a man with a plan, for us, for our life together.

From day one of my marriage, I'm a perfect wife. Steeped in how to please a man from my Practice House days in college, I could easily live in Stepford. Not only am I a good wife, I'm also a great teacher. Mediocrity has no place in my life. My teaching assignment is an inner-city high school in Syracuse, New York. Now I'm a country girl with a Catholic woman's college degree, and I know nothing about minorities. When I ask Betty Jones to read, she throws back her shoulders, glares at me, and says,

"I ain't gonna read and you ain't gonna make me."

If Betty Jones had been standing when she spoke, she would have towered over me, and I don't confront, ever. I would later find out that Betty is fourteen and has two children at home. I learn that Betty Jones doesn't know how to read. While this knowledge shocks me, I understand that in Betty's world reading is not a priority. What is important is something I am about to teach her—how to rely on your own judgment, not what others think is best for you.

The vehicle for this life lesson is sewing. She learns how to read as she follows the instructions for making darts in those tight skirts she likes so much. She comes to school for one reason only—to learn something she values. Her English teacher stops me one day in the hall and says, "I'd like to thank you for something. I have Betty Jones in first period and the only reason she comes to my class is because she has you second period."

I teach Betty for three years as she designs her own line of clothes and her self-esteem blossoms. She starts to make great decisions in her own best interest. My classes overflow with minority students who want to learn the skills they believe will help them in life. I become known as The Fox, whatever that means. I do know it's a compliment. "Good morning, Ms. Fox," they chime as they gather their fabrics and patterns.

The night before my class, I prepare my lesson on sewing darts. When my students come into class, I give a demo, explain they are to make their darts and then take them to the assessment table where I have placed the A+ darts, the perfect darts I had sewn the night before as examples. Each student will self-assess their darts against the A+ on display. I never have to be the judge. They know when they have the A+ and they know how to rip out.

Not everyone needs to sew the perfect dart—that isn't the point. What is important is for my students to begin to learn to trust their own judgments. In their lives they would have many tests; most of them would not be darts. The time they spend with me helps them understand how important their own decisions are to their future. Darts are only there for the tight skirts.

After three years my teaching ends and I become a mother. I have a son and we name him after his father; he's the joy of my life. His easygoing nature makes me the envy of others. They think I'm a perfect mother. I know I'm not perfect but I keep getting credit for my son's disposition. We visit family who have vowed never to have children. Just one day with our son and they muse, "Well, if we were sure our child would be like yours, we would reconsider."

Now we are blessed with our second child. I'm in love and she's barely two days old. Her hair is dark like mine and I'm sure she's going to be a beautiful, brown-eyed girl. When she looks up at me, she seems to be asking me to keep her safe. I already love her but that safety thing I struggle with. I'm haunted by thoughts I won't be able to manage two children, fearful I'll be less than perfect.

Before I can get up my resolve, my mother and my sister Liz walk into my hospital room. Liz is all ooo's and ahhh's as I introduce my baby girl Maya.

"What kind of name is that?" barks my mother.

I know exactly what she's getting at—Italian? I'm thinking more French than Italian, but I can't let it ride. I retort,

"Mom, it's Italian—it matches her last name." And then I lie, "In fact, she is named after her great-grandmother Mayabella, on her father's side."

My mother is stunned and speechless, which is a rare occurrence. My daughter and my mother would later connect through their mutual love of art, and their bond would be strong right up until my mother's death.

In the meantime, my perfection starts to show some blemishes. The first night home from the hospital I turn on the baby monitor and go upstairs to bed. When I wake up the next morning at seven, I check the monitor and the light is off. I panic, grab my robe, and run down the steps. When I enter Maya's room, she's lying there wide awake, not making a sound. Did she cry in the night? Did I hear her cry and reach over and turn the machine off? Could I do something like that? The next night, I sleep fitfully, waiting for her cry. She never cries once the entire night. I tiptoe into her room at 6:45 and she is sound asleep. She sleeps eight hours a night from that very first night.

I soon learn why my daughter sleeps so well. Maya is a spitfire. Full of spunk and determination, her dark brown ringlets bounce up and down as she shouts her very first word, "Mine, it's mine." And so, we settle down with a family fit for the royals: husband, wife, boy, and girl.

Now I focus on being a full-time homemaker. Every Sunday I take the newspaper grocery ads and plan our meals for the week. The specials become my entrees. Side dishes are chosen for a colorful plate just as we were taught in our foods and nutrition classes. I become a gourmet cook, hosting other foodies and newcomers to the neighborhood. As I'm preparing escargot, my son slips his hand in and grabs a morsel. Already a gourmand, he tells the waiter when we go out to eat, "I'd like to have one of those fillet things like my dad."

Always cute, he knows just how to get what he wants, he uses humor and tact. My daughter doesn't like gourmet food. Trying to keep her in her crib longer in the morning, I place a bowl of fruity cereal—yes, the sugary kind—in her crib before I go to bed. Perfect mom? Highly doubtful. Later when I'm working in retail and learn how to compute the sugar content of cereals, I am aghast at what I've done. When we go out to eat, her favorite food is fried clams. Clearly her mother is not perfect.

Being a Virgo, I need a plan with direction and organization. We will always follow our plan until my mother's warning comes to fruition. The boy who was abandoned when he was three will show up at the oddest times. Tonight, he's in our bedroom: We're dressing to go to a party, and my husband looks me over and says snidely,

"You're not going to go dressed like that, are you?"

It's Christmas and I have on black velvet jeans and a white silky shirt, adorned with satin epaulets on the shoulders. I think I look pretty good. The blouse has long sleeves and it's not revealing at all, so this can't be about me looking too sexy. I'm confused.

"Don't I look OK?" I say meekly.

"Don't you have any pride?" he sneers, cutting right through the silky fabric of my blouse and directly into my heart. "Don't you care what you look like, Katherine?"

Now it's late and I'm completely and utterly reduced to Little Kat, not good enough for the suitcase, not pretty enough to take to a party... The epaulets on my blouse are sliding down my shoulders, there's a gaping hole in my chest, my sleeves are down over my hands, and my beautiful hair is covering my face. From somewhere deep, a place I rarely go, I gather my courage and declare, "I'll go the way I am." Maybe I'm still a rebel.

We get in the car and no one speaks. At the party I have a couple drinks when a guy comes up to me and says, "Are you a swimmer?" Oh crap, must be the epaulets. He's not stopping, he keeps on, leaning closer. "You have the shoulders of a swimmer." Time to go. My husband grabs my hand and leads me out the door.

"Don't think you're going to come on to guys when I'm standing right there," he warns.

No way, I'm easily cowed. "You're wrong," I say. "I was just standing there innocently minding my own business."

When I can open the paper bags, I see I was "hot" and possibly even beautiful. That outfit with the epaulets made my shoulders stand out and then there were the velvet jeans.

My husband didn't want me to know how good I looked. He feared I'd leave him if I ever figured it out. He was afraid that by looking good I'd attract another man's attention. His fear would destroy us. My fear of confrontation would clinch the destruction. My mother knew. What you fear the most will be in the driver's seat.

My mother's fear that I would leave her would come true. My husband's fear-driven words would force me to abandon him and his worst fear would be realized. I would be the one to say stop. It would take me thirty-four years of marriage to finally say it.

"I deserve to be treasured. I am lovable."

We will cruise around in low gear, sometimes in high when we relocate for jobs and have to scramble to buy and sell houses, but we persevere in our tight little family unit. It isn't until I start to work and my husband loses his job that the union starts to come unglued.

A dalliance on my husband's part, a reluctance to follow him to a new job on my part, and our path comes to a crossroad. I'm working at a department store demonstrating small appliances and handing out samples and recipes to customers. My husband is working on his career plan. We are beginning to move in different directions. I'm becoming more independent and starting to have my own opinions. I'm also the number two salesperson in the store.

My husband goes to a coaching conference for a weekend, and when he comes back, he's acting weird and says he has something he needs to tell me. We are in the bedroom when he says, "I did something stupid last night. I was with a woman and things got carried away. I'm so sorry, I would never hurt you in any way. It just happened. It means nothing."

Now I have no time to rehearse anything, so I turn and walk out of the room. I'm going to need time to figure out how I feel about this, but I don't cry. I never cry. And I rarely let any feelings show. When I stop and get curious, I realize I'm not really surprised by his betrayal. We haven't been all that close lately. What I see is ammunition I can use against him and I start to fantasize a life for myself; one that doesn't include him.

He's supposed to begin a new job next month and I decide I'm not going—I'll stay here with the kids; he can go ahead on his own. We go our separate ways but he's persistent and rents a big house we can live in together while we try to work things out. Now I need to be practical since I can't afford to stay in our current house with what I make at the department store. It never occurs to me I could force him to pay for my house—I don't think like that.

I decide if I can find a great job in the new city, I'll go. The store has just named me the top salesperson and while they don't want to lose me, they're willing to transfer me to the new location. I stay for the sake of the family unit and the children, but I stay in name only. And I never confront, never ask for what I need.

"I know just what you need," he whispers, "some of Pappy's Pork."

Right—he has absolutely no idea what I need. I'm beginning to wonder if this is some kind of Italian lovemaking ritual, a type of honey-dripping foreplay. If this is some kind of pre-sex talk, about pork and pork products, even my friend Dora Jane and all her Southern charm is not going to be turned on by the promise of a pork injection.

Where has this wooing technique been honed and what is the appropriate response to such a generous offer? I'm tempted to yell out "soooooweeee" to bring some levity or release the tension I feel inside, but even humor won't stop the bile coming up in the back of my throat.

The promise of pork weaves through relocations both north and south. It's offered from rooftops and shouted from upstairs bedrooms. There are times it's accompanied by cold hard cash left on my bedroom dresser. My shame comes out of the bags and grabs for the bills. When I get curious, I see my deviant behavior—the actions of a prostitute. I take the money, pull back my shoulders, take a deep breath, and work on my perfect smile.

There are days when we love each other but there's always an undercurrent of unease. Something sets him off, he gets angry, someone makes a mistake—there are to be no mistakes. Walking on eggshells is the preferred method of moving around the house. I perfect it. I also excel in the art of nonconfrontation. We never talk about it.

Kat comes out and covers her head with her blue satin quilt. Remember Kat? She lost her voice that day, under that quilt. She's not coming out from under the satin anytime soon. All you need to do is raise your voice, and she heads for cover. All you have to say is, "You're not going out looking like that, are you?" and she is back there, on the back porch with her beggar's paper bags.

Consumed by life, raising children, working in retail, generally getting by, maybe an occasional vacation accompanied by a pork buffet, and time gets away from me. My sister Liz offers me a trip to California, and I leap at the chance. The kids are teenagers and busy with athletics and friends, so they don't accompany me. Liz is in school, getting a master's in therapy, and she decides to try out some of her new techniques on me.

After I've been running on for twenty minutes about my life, she asks the fateful question:

"But what do you need?"

"Who? Me? Can't think of anything at all. I have everything I…" I can't even finish the sentence when I realize no one ever asked me that before. Worst of all, I never asked me that before. And the absolute worst part is, I have no idea what I need.

The questions change my life. I write in my journal and as I think about my own needs, I'm curious if other women are like me—do they also struggle with what they want? Or are they "needless," as I suspect is a description of me. I doodle in the margins of my notebook; I draw a man and a woman with a bathroom scale between them. Then I script the words Needless to Say.

An idea starts to form in my mind—a book—about women's needs and fulfillment. The opening scene shows me in my casket. I'm draped in the blue satin quilt but I'm not dead. There's a glimmer, a spark, a beat; my sister Liz notices. At home I'm called selfish because I want something for myself, and my sister is scorned.

"Hippie-dippie liberals in California, they know nothing," my husband asserts.

I suggest we get some help with our marriage. My husband is reluctant, but I make it mandatory. "If we don't see a counselor, I'm going to leave."

Now he's confused in couple's therapy and asks, "What happened? I don't understand what happened. I thought we were ok, just fine." And we were "fine." Somewhere along the way "fine" was not enough for me.

I wonder about this idea for a book and I pursue my needs: to be authentic, to write, to learn, to laugh, to love, to be capable of loving myself. In my quest to love myself, I leave behind a house, enough stuff to fill a house, stability, insurance, and a love I could never satisfy—a little boy who wanted so desperately to be loved.

We're in the family room and I'm freezing. When I turn up the thermostat, I'm met with derision.

"I pay the bills in this house and I decide if the heat is turned up or down," declares my husband.

"Is that so," I sneer, ever so slightly confrontational. "How would you like it if someone spoke to you like that," I parry, now full-blown in his face. He answers with this rehearsed Italian refrain,

"Everything I have ever done I have done for this family—it's all I've ever wanted," and violins begin to play in the background.

"Is that right," I challenge. "Well, your stepfather is sitting there on the couch, the one you are sitting on right now, and he has just said those exact words to you, about doing everything for the family. Can you hear him? He has answered you in those exact words when you asked him why he didn't love you. Was his answer enough? The 'I did all of this for you'— was that enough?"

Stopping my diatribe, he begins to declare in almost a whisper, "No," he says. "It wasn't enough, I wanted him to love me."

It has taken me thirty-four years to break through the bravado, the anger, the pain, and all the requests for pork sandwiches. Maybe if I had learned to confront years ago, we might have had a chance but it's too late now.

"I did all of this for you, for my family," never did cut it for me. It always felt like sad-sacking. "Poor me, I've tried everything, given you everything."

But your stepfather never gave you the love your little boy deserved. Because you never got it from your family of origin, you couldn't give it to Kat, who never got it from her family and on and on, circles and circles. Somewhere, sometime tonight, someone is getting Pappy's pork injection and is loving every minute of it. I lose my taste for pork and discard the blue satin quilt. Eyes wide open, I discover I am lovable, and I learn how to turn on my own thermostat.

CHAPTER 9
Persistence

Journal Entry: June 10

 The lens I view the world through may have some wavy lines; like the glass you see in older houses; there are distortions. Accounting for the skewed vision, my mind continually searches for truth. How do I see the truth if my window to the world has cracks or wavy lines? Maybe what I need is a tool. Drawing the problem then turning it upside down lets me see the scale between me and my husband and, instead of separating us, it keeps us together.

 When you're perfect, your judgment of others is swift and deadly. You're right, correct, logical in your thinking. When you speak, all discussion ends. Succinct, absolute and dripping with venom you dare anyone to challenge you. If they do, you have data to back yourself up. I'm now starting to wonder why I would have to be so right all the time. And then I get a glimpse of my paper bags and the shame spilling out of them. Perfection, the twin of shame, mirror images. One covers up the other. The only way out is vulnerability, openness, and awareness. I need to stop the judging before I sling the arrows.

❖

No amount of time is too long to work on something. Nose to the grindstone, get it done. A gift from my mother. I'd say "tirelessly," but that would not be true; my mother was always tired. Five children, full-time job, and she had to somehow keep the white gloves white and the hats stacked in a hatbox. Yes, we had hatboxes and a dress form so my mother could drape fabric across her inert mail-order body double. Not everyone has a replica of their mother standing in the bedroom. Most of the time it was used as a hall tree, loaded with discarded dresses. This form was rigid, unbending, and always there when you thought you might go in your mom's drawer to nose around or even cop a few coins.

We bought our groceries at a market where my mom ran a tab. When we needed something, we just walked to the store, made our selection, and said, "Charge it." There was never cash around. Everything was paid by check. At Christmas each of us received one big gift bought the night before at the hardware store. My sister and I used to sit at the top of the steps and look through the railing as the gifts were laid under the tree. Ice skates for Our Jerry and me, baseball mitt for Joey, wagon for Eddie, and a doll for Liz.

It was magical to sit with my sister and watch our gifts being lovingly presented. Our Christmas tree was another thing altogether. Mom would leave the house with her saw and Our Jerry in tow. Together they would climb the mountain behind our house in search of the perfect tree. As we got older, the trees got weirder, but Mom was determined she would not buy a tree when there was a whole mountain behind our house.

Determination, persistence, and downright pluck describe my mother succinctly. The best part is she bestowed these gifts on all of us. In turn, my children are heirs to this legacy, although their spouses wonder sometimes if it's not a curse. Dogged determination belongs to pit bulls; when it's in your own DNA and it's midnight and you're still trying to get the disposal unstuck, those around you start to wonder. I cannot give up on an unfinished project. Here's the good news for you: I won't give up on you either. That same persistence takes me thirty-four years to finally say to my husband, "I'm afraid I'm going to have to give up, to give something up—you."

Love requires determination. It needs at least the level of persistence as the midnight garbage disposal. No one would say I gave up too soon. Sometimes when the grinder is stuck, no amount of time, or tool, or technique will do. There was one person, however, who did not think I should give up on my marriage—my mother. You see, she had never given up.

"Vows are for life," she would chide me. Maybe my curious self should have parried with, "I didn't give up on you Mom, little Kat with the ringlets, with the flouncy dresses and the white collars; little Kat with the paper bags, not good enough for your suitcase. I never gave up on you, Mom, I couldn't, I was just a kid." But then, what would be the point. My decision was mine alone.

My need to be perfect takes me to a place I barely understand—the know-it-all, the bigmouth, the show-off. "Have you ever been wrong?" friends would jibe me. Well, there was this once... After a while the perfection becomes a burden. Have to be right, can't keep my mouth shut, all-knowing; lately I've even been dispensing medical advice. Shameful, I know the perfection is shame-based. If I uncover the shame, can I stop the perfection? Apparently, I've not mined the shame deeply enough because knowing the twins—perfection and shame—has not stopped the need to be the star.

Vulnerability is the key and even though my heart is open to love there's still a part that self-protects, a part I won't let anyone see. Who is she and what does she have to hide? I've admitted the unworthiness and the paper bags, but that must be just the tip of the iceberg. What is it the showman wants? To be loved, acknowledged, accepted—to belong? Ooohhh, just felt a pinch there. I've always had a certain pride in not needing anyone—a self-reliance. If you're perfect, you don't need anyone or anything.

Growing up, I remember my mom warning us against friends.

"They'll hurt you and talk about you behind your back. Friends are not to be trusted. It's better not to let anyone get close."

And so, my mom never did have friends. She would say things like,

"Women are snide and gossipy, I prefer men."

It's hard for me to believe my mother's warnings about friends would have had any effect on me. I barely listened to anything she had to say. Is it possible that the undercurrent of antisocial leaning could have affected me in such a way that I would push people away and become so perfect as to not be approachable as friend material?

I do have a close friend, Belle. We bonded over jobs and men. At the time we hated both. Commiseration sealed our friendship. Belle and I are both in the consumer affairs business. My job is located in the store while Belle is in the community, planning parties sponsored by appliance companies. Nonprofit groups are the recipients of Belle's parties and the idea is to showcase all the latest in kitchen appliances, ovens, mixers, gadgets. Food vendors supply the ingredients, the nonprofits supply the workers, and Belle demonstrates all the latest cooking techniques creating delicious recipes. The nonprofits sell tickets for the parties at a nominal price and keep the proceeds.

The department store promotes me to director of consumer affairs, which is one of those jobs like human relations, not directly related to the bottom line. Without my sales to boost me up, my position is tenuous. When recession hits, my job is eliminated. Now the person I call is not my husband, it's Belle. As we clean out my office, she spies a box of rubber gloves and proceeds to blow them up and position each with the middle finger sticking right up in the air. Belle is an irreverent rebel—the best antidote to my perfectionism.

While the idea for Belle's job is a no-brainer, store managers and appliance vendors start to cool on the demonstrations, and she is on the chopping block. We both realize customer service jobs do not directly bring in money. If you're to keep your job, you have to have some way to be seen as an asset. In my dealings with the retail associations, I come across a formula for computing our worth:

Each satisfied customer (A) = $

Number of customers satisfied through Belle's program (B)

A x B = $$$.

And, yes, there is a dollar amount a satisfied customer brings in any industry. When we figure her worth, the number is staggering.

With my encouragement and Belle's irreverence, we develop a plan; a letter goes to the director of marketing for the appliance manufacturer. I will never forget the look on her face when her program is accepted. Not only will she make a nice salary, the money will boost her social security.

I don't have a lot of friends. I keep to myself, cover it with a writer's need for solitude. But it's more than that. I have secrets. We're not what we appear; we're not a model family. It's all a sham. I've spent years perfecting the illusion. When you're scrambling trying to look perfect, even just a crack in the facade will throw everything off.

Now I wonder how the perfection will withstand a gaping fissure—newspaper headlines about a suicide pact on my son's baseball team—where my husband is the head coach. There is no way I can pretend or hide this fact—*USA Today*, the newspaper people, are in my front yard.

Tightly controlled, woven together so tensely with the warp yarns it's impossible to allow the weft thread to pass through; this is my life. While I never use a loom to help me weave, I create a cloth so taut the ideal frame I build around my family is beginning to fray.

We send the kids to stay with friends so they don't have to answer reporters' questions when they go out their front door. Years later my daughter will wonder,

"Tell me if this happened—did you send us away when the suicide pact was going on?"

At the time, our facade is cracked wide open and neither of us do what is best for our children. We should hold them close, envelop them in love, but we are in full-out survival mode. You don't learn how to deal with the news media in home economics.

Our lives are on display for all to see, local tv, national tv, newspapers, the only thing missing is the internet—too early for Facebook. A child has died, and others are to follow. This is a bedroom community in an upper-middle or some will call lower-upper income bracket. Dirty laundry is not aired. Twelve-year-olds sign chits at the country club, sixteen-year-olds drive Z's and cars with alphabet letters, and eighteen-year-olds take their lives for no apparent reason. If trouble is brewing no one really wants to know.

Earlier this year, my son asks me if he can have a coed sleepover. It's asked with such candor, my response is, "First you will have to call every parent of every kid on your list and get their approval. If they agree, then it's ok with me." He gets halfway through his list and decides it's all too much trouble.

This is a child who can sell anything. At seventeen he buys a Cutco set of knives with a plan to go door to door. We figure this will be a great lesson in humility. Later that night I ask him how he did. He looks me in the eye, blinks a couple times, and the edges of his lips turn up just slightly, and in an aw-shucks tone of voice he says, "I only sold $1,800 worth of knives." Maybe I should send my son out front to deal with the reporters.

The rumored suicide pact has a date and time—the regional baseball playoffs. While most kids put on their uniforms with proud parents shooting pictures, there will not be playoff games for my son's team. They forfeit and someone has to take the fall: the guy at the top, the head coach, my husband. Repercussions of the stress include angioplasty, new medications, increased instability, not to mention the chasm we find ourselves looking into which was once a tightly knit union.

Our son loses two more friends to suicide, and many wonder how such a nightmare can take place in our little hamlet. None of us know then that the tightly woven threads, that core of support, are stretched too thin and they won't be able to withstand any new stress or tension. Our warp and weft strands come undone and not even the best weaver, clothmaker or home economist is able to hold the fibers firmly enough; they loosen, and the fabric of our union unravels.

CHAPTER 10
Courage

Journal Entry: September 15

We are living in Albany where my husband takes a position after losing his job when the suicide pact occurs. I'm in the process of interviewing women for my book "Needless to Say" and I decide to attend a meeting where Phyllis Brown, family and consumer sciences supervisor, is the speaker. In her keynote, she states,

"Family and consumer sciences (FCS), previously called home economics, will be at the forefront of the movement to content standards. We will be forging the steel for the rails that will be the foundation of the new direction in education. Some educators will get on the train, some will miss the train, but we will be laying the tracks. Our teachers will go back to their home school districts and become the leaders. We will have standards for FCS and we will not only be included, we will be at the forefront of the change."

I stay after the meeting to introduce myself to this passionate educator, Phyllis. She tells me to call her Phil, and I can see she is a visionary. She is also politically connected: the sister of a congressman. I would be so impressed by the words of this educational leader, I would volunteer to help her gather the steel we would need for the train tracks.

The room goes dark and the screen on the stage lights up. All I see are fire and elephants. What kind of a seminar is this? And why aren't the animals trying to get away from the flames? They're just standing there while the fire rages all around them. But, clearly, there's nothing hindering their escape—no shackles, no ropes, nothing. Then the screen goes blank.

Phyllis Brown introduces a team of graduate students in psychology who begin to explain the video we've just seen.

"The animal trainers start with the baby elephants by tying their feet with ropes. The young animals resist and pull but over time give up because they're not strong enough to get free. When they become adults and could easily break the ropes, they don't even try, they just accept their fate. Even when the circus tent catches fire, the elephants don't try to save themselves; they believe they're still tied to the posts."

My ankles are starting to itch and my hand is starting that twitching thing I do when I get anxious. My breathing's ragged and I'm starting to sweat. I'm not feeling well—I'm in the video—I'm the elephant. I'm trapped and the tent is on fire. The screen lights up again with the words *Learned Helplessness.*

Now, the presenters have my full attention and my breathing calms as I hear about a new concept in psychology, regarding a learned response—*helplessness.* In the audience are the teacher trainers who will take this new information back to their home districts. I'm part of the advisory team putting together strategies to move home economics into the twenty-first century. In this effort, we need to help teachers break those invisible ropes that bind them to old, ineffective ways of thinking. Elephants get the point across nicely.

Phyllis calls this the "Train the Trainer" model and it's the first step of laying down the steel for the train tracks; the forging of the metal. Our teachers will need to be strong and confident. The team focuses on tips for helping students who may show signs of this malady: students who give up easily, who have already decided they aren't smart enough, good enough, quick enough to learn. Students who could easily break the ropes but are tethered to a self-concept that shows they're defeated before they even try. While the presenters focus on students, it's the teachers in the audience, the trainers, who fill out the questionnaires.

In my mind I'm still in the tent but the fire is out and I've survived. Would I survive another fire, another crisis? I'm exactly like the adult elephants that refuse to even try to get free, and to make it worse, I see it as someone else's problem. Someone is unhappy with me so I'm fearful and decide I have no choice. I couldn't get free even if I wanted. And I'm sure this will always be true. Others might have the power to leave but not me; my leg bands are firmly affixed.

Part of our seminar is a series of questions about our inclinations when faced with problems. How do we usually react? Do we blame others? See issues as all-consuming? Problems only for me but not for others? The profile I create from the questionnaire is shocking. I'm clearly a person with learned helplessness. Lucky for me, the presentation is going to give me ways to help students become more positive and overcome what is chillingly described as a pathway to a lifetime of depression.

What I find out is my writing saves me. Because I'm able to get my thoughts and fears down on paper, I've taken steps in a positive direction. And while I've not taken any action whatsoever to change my situation, the fact that I thought about it and wrote it down was enough to keep me from falling into malaise.

I save myself, but I don't really make progress. I have to Train the Trainers and act as if I know exactly how to help teachers learn to recognize students who feel helpless. This is good practice for me because all the while I'm learning, getting stronger, more proactive, more focused on refuting the words in my head that say,

"You'll never be good enough, you're a beggar, you're not going out dressed like that, are you?"

In the training sessions, I learn to reframe my thinking so that one situation doesn't set the tone for everything that follows. Just because I've had a setback in one area of my life doesn't mean the whole world is moving in the same direction. I have a long way to go but I've found the best way to begin is to write.

I'm convinced courage skipped me and went straight from my mom to my daughter. Now this concept of courage has reared up again in my life and I'm fighting it with everything I have: intellectualism, logic, even elephants—anything other than what it really is—time to stand for what I believe. I've lived my whole life in fear—fear of what others think, fear that I'm not good enough.

I'm wondering if what I fear is that I am, in fact, too much. I know I'm smart and have a good mind, but would I try to stay small in order to fit in, to belong? Is my need to be loved so great I would forsake the essential me? I've never lived up to my potential. Just like my dad who routed trucks around New York, I've skirted around issues of nutrition, addiction, health, and happiness. Even though I'm curious, I never try to remove the shackles. Like the elephants, the invisible ropes keep me tied to the paper bags and the traumatic experiences of my childhood.

While forging the steel for the rails is a team effort, the job of removing the shackles from my ankles is mine alone. I find courage buried deep—a video with elephants and fire—and a message of hope.

My book on "women's needs" morphs into a consulting job and I work with school districts using a problem solving technique I honed for the book.

Phil invites me to have lunch with her brother at the United States Capital Building. At lunch we discuss big ideas.

I'm taken by the way the congressman is completely present. Phil's brother doesn't look around or get sidetracked—he gives us his full attention—even when he's told Clint Eastwood is downstairs wanting an audience. This is surely a test. When we're finished with lunch, Phil and I hang around to see if we can spot Clint but are ushered out by the aides.

Today, we may not be able to affect national education priorities, but we've opened a dialogue for spirited discussion to begin. As we exit the government building, I leave with a newfound feeling of legitimacy. I'm among thinkers, big thinkers. I may have something to offer, something of worth.

CHAPTER 11
Attachment Trauma

Journal Entry: May 8

I've been covering you up and not letting you come out and be beautiful. Why do I do that? Am I afraid I'll have to shake things up if I let myself be pretty? What am I afraid of? Somehow the weight must be working for me, keeping me down, not letting me shine. What am I getting from being fat? Is it an excuse not to have to care about myself? A reason to berate myself, a self-fulfilling prophecy? Am I worthy of love? Am I a worthy recipient of my own love?

I'm disappointed you can't stand up for yourself. How could you not know how beautiful and therefore how threatening you are? Can you let it all go and let love, as imperfect as it is, into your heart?

Sheila, Phil, and I decide to go back to my house to chill out after one of our teacher training sessions. Sheila is in the process of getting certified as a craniosacral therapist and she needs someone to practice on. Phil declines but I agree to give it a try. Sheila explains,

"Craniosacral therapy is a form of bodywork that uses a series of gentle touches and follows the rhythm of the spinal fluid from the base of the spine to the head. It can help reduce stress and other tensions."

I like the sound of this, I'll be Sheila's very first victim—ahhh, I mean—her test case, her first touch, her patient. As we enter my bedroom, I'm pulling back the tent flap on a Native American ceremony as it is about to begin. With just a glimpse of the healer Sheila, I picture her surrounded by beautiful women in colorful beaded dresses and spectacular feathers. Here with my friends, I'm safe and loved, like the whole tribe is watching over me.

Sheila has a lovely voice and speaks softly, reassuring me by explaining how we work together energetically.

"I listen to your body and what my fingers tell me as I touch your head and neck. We tune in to each other's rhythms and energy. You can let go and trust me. I am here with you. You're safe here in this room."

Sheila asks me to lie down on my bed, the single bed I've been sleeping in lately. As I lie on my back, my hands folded across my stomach, she puts a hand under my back to support me. "There are always two hands on the body, one supporting the body underneath and the other can be under the chin, under the head, on top of the heart—this is to have the energies conducted between the therapist and the patient," Sheila explains almost in a whisper.

Her touch is wonderful, very soothing. Sheila is talking about the soft tissue and the movement of the fluid around my neck and spine. She says she can tell how much resistance there is by how firm or soft the tissues are. This is fascinating. Then my body starts to let go; I see the native women surround me as love enters the room.

I'm in a garden; there are beautiful roses everywhere. They're climbing on vines. I want to tell Phil what she's missing, but I don't seem to be able to speak. Now the vines are growing too fast; they're out of control. There's definitely something wrong with my throat. I start to get fidgety, and I think I'm moaning but I'm not sure any of it's real. Then my hands come up off my stomach and reach for my neck. I'm grabbing at my neck now, frantic to pull something away, something keeping me from being able to talk, something that is now stopping my breath. Oh God, I can't breathe. We have to stop.

Q, who is always present and as close to me as possible, puts her paw on my leg. As I start to talk, Sheila puts her hands on my shoulders, to reassure me, to calm me down. Then my breathing starts to slow. I have to talk. I need to tell Sheila about the vines.

"There were vines around my throat, choking me. I couldn't pull them off. They were trying to kill me. Choking the life from me, and I couldn't stop it," I say, trying to pull myself together. "Do you think this happens for other people when they do this therapy?"

"Different people have different reactions," says Sheila. "Craniosacral therapy encourages your body's natural ability to heal itself. Figuring out where the pain resides in your body is the first step of healing."

Clearly the pain for me is in my throat. Maybe that's why I lose my voice, why I don't speak up, why I rehearse what I want to say a million times before I say it. Then there were those vines.

"Sheila, the vines had thorns. I think that's why it was so scary. I couldn't breathe, like I was being smothered."

And then the significance of the vines slams me in the face. I'm suffocating, in my marriage. The vines that surround my heart have grown up and out and are now circling my throat. My life force is being choked out.

Sheila tells me to breathe; she says, "What came up for you is emotions you have been keeping at bay, feelings you want to keep hidden. And they expressed themselves as thorns. You're talking to me so you are able to breathe, you are ok."

Once I can get calm, Sheila tells me sometimes the release of tension through craniosacral therapy allows your body to tell your brain what's going on. Usually, I ignore what my body is telling me and only listen to my brain. With this hands-on therapy, my body-pain asserts itself saying: *the inability to speak up for yourself is connected to the vines surrounding your throat.*

Anything that threatens my speech, including talking back, or standing up for myself is scary. Even though I don't want to talk about my marriage and never confront my husband, the craniosacral message is clear—I need to save my own life.

My husband and I will seek couple's counseling but will be roadblocked in our second session when our therapist asks each of us to describe our role models for love.

"You go first," I say, dripping sarcasm. Both stymied, we retreat to our childhood selves. "You never…" I start to say.

"You turned Maya against me," he says.

Our wise counselor asks us to bring a "picture of love" when we come for out next session. She wants us to go home and find a picture that says love, is a visual depiction of love.

I choose a picture of me as a little girl with my big brother, Our Jerry, as we hold hands and prepare to ditch our mother. My hair is dark brown with ringlets cascading down the back. The curls resemble rings of bologna that bob up and down when I run.

I'm dressed in a very feminine style with a full flouncy skirt and a proper white collar on my blouse. I'm overdressed for a romp in the yard, but even when I was three my mother insisted I look like a little lady. My hand is firmly clasped to my brother's, a union that will endure for the rest of our lives.

When we arrive for our session, our therapist asks about our pictures, which we lovingly describe. She never mentions the fact that the pictures we bring are not of the two of us in a loving pose together. Maybe she's saving that little piece of reality for another time.

The therapist tells us in order for us to work on our marriage, we each have to look at our childhoods. I know I have a lot of work to do if I'm ever to heal, so I grab my journal and start writing. My first memories of childhood trauma are those damn anal inspections. This is not going to be easy.

CHAPTER 12
Bravado

Journal Entry: August 12

My addictions were formed in my family. We all have them. My background includes the Irish (drinking) heritage. Personally, I'm addicted to food. If I use food in place of love, then I don't need love. I've substituted food for love.

There's nowhere I can hide. My feet start trembling and I'm squeezing my eyes shut. I don't want to hear this. I want to put my fingers in my ears and hide under my blue satin quilt. But there's no more quilt; threadbare and rotting, it was thrown away years ago. That quilt was my protector in this house with all the pretense and secrets. When I was a kid, I hid under that delicious rich fabric and would pretend I was somewhere else, someone else. The quilt won't help me now.

Our Jerry has called us all together. We are to meet at our house where my mother still lives. He wants to talk to us about something big, something he needs to discuss with all of us, including our mother. This never happens. We never tell Mom anything; she gets too aggravated and angry. She thinks people should mind their own business. What happens in our house stays in our house.

"No one needs to know our business," she declares.

This theme of "no one needs to know" is a pattern in our house. Our mother continually warns us about talking outside the house, confiding in others, telling other people our private business. I never got what she was talking about, but I did know the beatings were shameful. I never told anyone about the beatings.

We're seated in the living room: Mom, Our Jerry, me, and Eddie. Liz lives in California and can't be with us. Dad passed away; complications from a series of strokes that left him partially paralyzed, unable to communicate, and worst of all, they broke his brain. Toward the end of his life, my mother had to lock him in the bedroom at night so he wouldn't wander the house and get hurt. This nighttime ritual was heartbreaking to see.

My dad's great love was writing; his claim to fame, a piece in *Reader's Digest* under the heading "People Say the Darnedest Things." Years later, when we are cleaning out our family home after my mother's death, we find the novel Dad had been writing.

It's up in the cupboard over his desk, right beside his favorite book—a hollowed-out shell where he hid his booze. No wonder Dad's novel doesn't make any sense. He must have gone into his sanctuary, put a sheet of paper in the typewriter, opened the fake book, pulled out the whiskey bottle, taken a swig, and then began pecking away.

We figured he either had no talent or he was so tired when he did sit down at night to write, his sentences rambled on. When we open the faux book and see the empty bottle, it all makes sense—the disjointed sentences, the anger, the deep sense of failure, the unfulfilled potential. My mother must have known about the alcohol. Why didn't we all know?

The answer is chilling: we knew but we lived in a world of pretense—everything was fine.

Like Dad, my brothers become players. When they're teenagers, Joey and Eddie caddy at the local golf course and are highly sought after by older women because of their manners and good breeding—at least that's what my mother thinks. Neither one ever tell about the escapades when they're picked up in Cadillacs and whisked away. And as it will be, Dad starts playing golf. It's the highlight of his playing days—to be able to golf with his sons, a game he comes to love.

Joey and Eddie go on to win club championships in their local communities. Gambling stays in Joey's blood. In a golf game, he bets on a thirty-foot putt and walks away with his pockets full of cash. He parlays a high-risk venture into a thriving business.

Joey has what our mother calls "get up and go." His death comes as a great shock to us and the community that loves him. At forty-nine, a beloved doctor dies and the line around the funeral home goes on for blocks.

Our Jerry has called us together to discuss the coroner's report regarding Joey's death. He is secretive, mysterious, almost speaking in a whisper. I look around but Eddie won't make eye contact. He knows what Our Jerry is going to say. Mom is starting that twitching thing she does with her hands. Stop it, Mom, I want to say. Her eyes are darting around, daring anyone to say even a word. I start to look over my shoulder. Can the neighbors hear? Is it something bad?

When I catch my breath, I realize Our Jerry is still talking, something about "medical examiner" and "morphine." No, I'm not going to listen to this. I need to get up and walk away, someplace safe where I can just breathe.

"Kat," says Jerry, "are you all right?"

No, I'm not all right. I will never be all right again.

"You can go lie down if this is too much," he murmurs.

What about Mom? I look over and she's stoic. Gone somewhere else.

Not her family, not her boy, her Joey—the most successful of all of us. Big house, thriving medical practice, bastion of the community, and morphine? My mother raises her chin and says in her best Godfather voice,

"This will not destroy our family."

We keep coming back to Joey's retort when someone would ask him how he was doing. "If I was any better," he would begin to declare and we all agreed, we should have known, he was not ok. Not even in the slightest bit fine. The bravado was a telltale sign.

We lose our brother and I'm immobilized. Living on my couch in my four-bedroom house, I become obese. I don't leave the house. My sister Liz starts to pick at her face and Eddie sees conspirators everywhere. Our Jerry is held together by the love of a good woman, his wife Sandy. The rest of us divorce, not quite seeing the pattern of loss and pain.

Liz's divorce will be underwritten by the generosity of Joey's envelope full of cash, sent in the mail months before his death, without a word or a return address. She opens the letter and out fall the bills; no note, no signature.

Eddie is lost without the Frick of the Frick and Frack duo. In his sorrow, this most ethical lawyer stumbles and falls into deep depression. It takes us years to recover. Some of us do better than others. I write, Liz becomes a therapist and listens to another's pain, Our Jerry is a pillar of his community as their pharmacist and friend, and Eddie continues to work in wills and estates as his reputation for being honest garners him clients in need of a lawyer they can trust.

On Joey's death certificate, the medical examiner writes heart complications or something innocuous. I never really wanted to know what the official document said or if it was ever changed. When I open the paper bags now, I understand how important it was to my mother for the family to remain strong, to persevere. She knew we would need to keep our family bond tight. What she would never know is how desperately we would need the resilience in the years to come.

CHAPTER 13
Healing

Journal Entry: July 20

I've returned from Lilydale where I've gone to have a reading. In the past, I've accompanied my friend Lisa, who introduced me to her medium, Kitty. Now, I don't believe in all that aura stuff and the past lives so when it's my turn, I don't offer up one clue.

Lisa is a teacher so when Kitty asks me if I am also, I say no. She follows with, "That's interesting since you are surrounded with books—they are cascading down your shoulders."

Hmmm…. "Well," I concede, "I am a writer."

"That explains it then," says Kitty.

When she hears I'm in the process of retiring, she tells me she sees palm trees in my future, duh, like that's hard to predict. She did get my attention though when she said, "I have a good friend who wrote a story about a cat—Garfield—he might be able to help you if you need an agent or publisher."

Now I'm totally in sync with this wise woman, this seer, whose name is

Kitty and she is friends with a cat author who might be able to help me. And I can see why Lisa comes here. In fact, I'm going to bring my friends Phyllis and Sheila so they can get a reading too.

Sheila, Phyllis, and I decide to go to Lilydale, a spiritualist village in Western New York, for the day. We start our morning at the Healing Temple with a visit to the reiki healers, who offer a short complimentary session. I'm standing in line waiting for my turn when a kind of energy emanates from the front of the room. The healers don't seem to be touching anyone, only moving their hands above and around the heads and shoulders of the people in front of me.

What is this? I wonder if it's like craniosacral therapy, but there's no touching, rubbing, or massaging. I do have to admit, it has the exact same feel as the session with Sheila at my house. If I make my eyes squinty, I can almost see my tribe of women surrounded in love.

Now I step forward and close my eyes as suggested. My heart slows down and peace comes over me. I'm a skeptic so I want to fight it but there's no doubt, it's a powerful vibe. There's only one word—love. I don't even know this healer in front of me, but energy is flowing here. How can this be if there's no physical hands-on?

My curiosity is heightened along with my skepticism. My body is responding to this non-touch gift, but my brain is resisting. I wonder if this is another one of those experiences I've been having lately where my body is the knower—the part of me that cries, screams, and feels pain. Why do I resist?

Something is lurking here, something unknown, just below the surface of my consciousness. Something that only shows itself when I'm in certain places like yoga, meditation, craniosacral therapy, and now reiki. While I don't understand, I'm starting to see the pattern.

The more I get quiet, listen to my breath, calm down my mind, the easier I go into my body. So even if I can't speak of the unworthiness, I can sense it in my chest, or notice how my fingers start to clinch and my breathing gets ragged. The key to the whole mystery is to get quiet.

I'm relaxed and peaceful as we walk toward the Gathering Hall. This is an afternoon session where hundreds of people gather while the mediums come through one by one, picking people out of the audience supposedly at random. I'm gazing at my navel, keeping my head down so as not to be noticed, when all of a sudden Phyllis pokes me in the side and says, "I think they mean you."

"What?" I mumble.

"You in the purple sweater, I have someone who wants to speak to you. Someone departed."

Oh, just great—in front of hundreds of people, they pick me.

"I see someone needs to tell you something but it's not clear. He wants me to come back again, maybe later," says the seer.

Phew, that was close. False alarm. I go back to my navel gazing while the mediums pass through.

Just as I'm wondering how much lint has accumulated in my belly button, Phyllis whacks me again.

"Oh, it's definitely you," she warns.

Come on, folks, you got me already.

"Spirit has someone here. It's a man, an uncle or maybe a brother," announces the medium.

Great! Some dead relative decides now is the time to talk to me in front of all these people. An uncle? No, I can't think of anyone who would have an interest in me. Brother? Joey? My brother Joey? He always did have a sense of the dramatic.

"This man is concerned about your finances. He wants you to make sure whatever you do you will be able to take care of yourself."

Oh, it's about money? Gotta be Joey. He would be the one to worry about my financial future. He's worried about me—concerned that I won't have enough money to live on if I get divorced. Joey knows I've never lived on my own and he knows how important money is going to be. He's reaching out to me, trying to get me to be sure I get my fair share.

Joey never liked my husband. In fact, he barely tolerated him. One time when we had stopped to visit, something we rarely did, there was some kind of problem with how I had parked the car and my husband started berating me. I looked over at Joey and saw his body become rigid and his hands ball up into tight fists. I knew my brother had a temper, so I quickly stepped toward him, took his hands, unfurled his fingers, and led him away from the source of problem.

Now, I'm in this hall at Lilydale and my navel no longer interests me. What concerns me is the water dripping from my eyes. No way. I'm crying, in front of all these people. Crying for my brother who's gone, for my marriage that's over, for the little girl Kat who only ever wanted a loving, safe place. She's come to Lilydale to get a glimpse into her future and instead she gets pulled into the past.

"I see purple all around you," claims the third medium in succession who points me out to the crowd. "Purple is the color of healing. Your aura suggests you may be a healer yourself."

Right. Got it. Duh, it's the purple sweater, my aura is purple. Can't fool me. Now I'm a healer too. But this healing thing will have to work in reverse. Before I become this healer they speak of, I will need to heal myself.

CHAPTER 14
Curiosity

Journal Entry: October 10

As the vines grew over my heart and threatened to choke me, they grabbed for my throat. I could see it was the only way to save my life. You can't love if you can't breathe so I did the only thing I could—I cut the vine and let my heart be free.

I tell my husband I want to separate and go to the Keys by myself—live by myself—just me and Q. My husband and I are going to a therapist, so he's not surprised but he is very hurt and confused. He keeps asking what went wrong. I keep playing my Patsy Cline songs, the ones where she's walking and looking for love, and Roy Orbison, "In Dreams." They all have a certain melancholy.

The essence of a writer is a curious mind. When my daughter's therapist says, "I need to see your mother," I'm desperate to find all the curiosity I can muster, and I mumble to myself, "Great, just great, it's always the mother."

I make an appointment and the therapist tells me, "You did not take care of your problems with your husband—you let your daughter become your protector. Now your daughter comes to see me because she's angry and she wants to figure out why. Do you understand your part in her anger?"

I'm devastated. All the while I think I'm keeping peace in the house, but I'm really avoiding conflict with my husband. Reluctant to confront my own situation, I arm my daughter with guns and ammunition for war with her father. What should have been my fight becomes hers. This revelation destroys me. When I try to recall my complicity, a family scene comes to mind.

We are at the kitchen table having dinner, talking about current events, probably politics, when I disagree with my husband. Our family dinners are monologues since neither one of the kids say much; they just want to eat and head out the door and play with their friends. I rarely talk; I pride myself on being a good listener. Suddenly my husband turns on me after I've voiced my own opinion, saying, "When you make what I make, you can vote."

This denigration stops a fork in mid-air. I glare at my husband, but I don't say a word. I only pause briefly, don't even stop eating. If I had been more confident, I might have been able to ask one of the curious questions such as, "Do you want to have a relationship with me? If you do, this is not how you show it." As it was, I was cowed, unsure, and penitent.

Our children are sitting at the table. My son is not paying attention to the conversation and is probably thinking about baseball, so it goes right over his head. Our daughter's knife hits the table with a thud.

She turns to her father and says, "If you want to show us love and have us love you, this is not how it works." Twelve years old, she's the truth-teller, sound familiar?

When a child witnesses this treatment of her mother, a certain rage begins to simmer. My regret is that I didn't stand up for myself and my daughter became my protector, pulling her further away from any chance she might have had for a relationship with her father.

Years later, my husband accuses me of turning our daughter against him. In a way it's true although it wasn't conscious. Always trying to make peace, I'd tiptoe around for fear his anger would erupt and we'd all be sucked up into it.

Now, I'm curious why a mother would build a wall around her heart to keep out pain yet not realize she is also blocking out love?

I wonder how a daughter becomes her mother's champion and turns against her father?

How does the pretense of a perfect family affect a daughter who sees that no one tells the truth?

How does a boy avoid the truth of what is going on around him?

What happens to your communication skills and relationships when no one says what they mean?

Is this what happened to my brother Joey? He was the only one of us who defied my mother and yet it wasn't enough to save him from his demons. He wanted her love. His gut-wrenching accusation written on the back of Our Jerry's picture—*You love him more than me*—was a tragic plea for love. But in a house of pretense, such a show of pain is turned to ridicule.

I grew up in a house where I stood up for my mother and told the truth. I got beaten for it. That was the '50s and kids got hit. Now, looking back, I can see the similarities in my house of origin and the house where I raised my family. I never noticed it before. There was no hitting, but then no one had to hit me to get me to acquiesce. When I look at the above questions, curiosity and wonder make the similarities impossible to ignore.

Just like my mother, I blocked out love, kept a wall around my heart. I became my mother's champion and turned against my father. I pretended my marriage, and my family were perfect. And I never said what I meant or what I felt.

I did all of this to avoid confrontation. In my mind, confronting begets anger. I can't let anyone get angry with me. It's not logical, it's a perception. Anger terrifies me because I assume it brings with it a beating.

My dad's anger when I was growing up is always there in my mind. But there is a terror in me that defies reason. Rationally it makes no sense for me to be so scared. Part of it is the raised voice, but the main issue is the ranting and raving of someone completely out of control, that look when I knew my dad was gone, lost any sense at all of what he was doing to me.

Today, all you have to do is raise your voice, scream obscenities, and it doesn't even have to be directed at me. It can be turned toward the traffic, the flat tire, the effing technology—there might just as well be a target on my chest. And I'm back there, under the blue satin quilt.

When I get a glimpse in the paper bags, I see the shame—the little girl who got beautiful clothes but was beaten for telling the truth. I understand it was the '50s and everyone got strapped, whipped, knocked around, so why did I have to take it to the level of shame and then cover up the shame with its twin—perfection? The extremes of goodness and badness somehow confused me, and I had nowhere to go to discuss my options.

There were always those who were more than willing to help me find my way. "I can help you feel better like this…" Those feelings, however great in the moment, only made me more confused. Now I couldn't even trust my own thoughts and decisions, and the choice to be perfect seemed the only way to go.

The irony is I was never perfect. I was a pretense and a fake, but I was good at it. No one knew, no one guessed. It wasn't until my daughter's therapist said, "You did not take care of business between you and your husband and you let your daughter be your protector"—what kind of mother would do that?

I seem to have no other choice now. As I polish my teeth, grinning into the mirror, I will make a first impression that is memorable. "You have a beautiful smile," people will say. When I am obese, people will comment on my beautiful face. When my Italian husband is queried by his family about why he would choose someone who is not model-thin, he says, "She has the most beautiful smile in the world."

Maybe my mother was right when she said the first thing men look at is your smile and your teeth. And so, I hone my incisors. But I'm not smiling now. My facade is chipped and cracked wide open. I let my daughter fight my battles because I refused to confront, to be less than perfect, to talk back, to disagree. I was so afraid of the anger that might ensue or the barrage of put-downs, I kept my perfect demeanor and let my daughter put on the armor and go to war on my behalf.

I did all this unconsciously, all the while thinking what a perfect mother I was. I walk around the house, terrified I'll step on a land mine. When I look back, I have no idea how I was able to pull off the facade for all those years—you'd think my heart would have given out for all the stress I put it under. And then there's my daughter, my courageous daughter. There's no way I can ever make any of it up to her—it changed who she is and it changed how she sees the world.

Curiosity is the only way I can approach what I did in the name of keeping the peace. I will search in the paper bags and I'll ask myself the questions. I pray I'll be loved because I'm human and vulnerable and imperfect. I will always struggle with perfection as it is locked onto my soul.

I come from a long line of self-medicators, self-prescribers, do-it-your-self shrinks. My self-diagnosis is fear of my own anger. Here's the visual:

I'm dressed in black leather, huge silver belt buckle pulled tight to hold all the rage inside. Black streaks outline my cheekbones and I'm holding a picture of the little girl with her ring bologna curls. Her hands are tightly squeezed, she's looking around furtively, trying to find a place to hide, someplace safe.

That's all she ever wanted: love and a safe place. Suddenly the buckle starts to split open from all the pent-up anger and there's nothing to stop it. It's the "nothing to stop it" I fear. My self-prescription is a heaping tablespoon of rage, spewed from my lips in such a way that it blows away my bologna curls and unfurls my fingers so they can make huge threatening gestures.

But what does this do to my need for a safe place? Maybe I should join a theater troupe so I can play those juiciest of parts like Joan Crawford in *Mommy Dearest*. Maybe not, too close to home.

When you're nice, known as friendly and likable, you have a reputation to keep up. I've been veering from my niceness lately with edginess and sarcasm. Maybe this is my circuitous route to anger. Like an inchworm I'm crawling along—a little snide remark here, a caustic comment there. But a powerful emotional tirade? I can't seem to muster the energy for it. Passive-aggressive, I'm wondering? What about a full-blown frontal attack? Where would I direct my anger? I should be angry at me, the mother who had her daughter suit up for war.

Do I need to make amends to the little girl? Maybe I can explain to her this curiosity idea, how together she and I might heal by wondering about parents and the times in which they lived.

I just keep on dragging those paper bags along. Time to rip them open, lean my lips in, and blast away with every ounce of energy I can gather. If I can't be on Broadway, my paper bags will suffice for my soliloquies. The best part of the perfect paper bag rant is when you're done, you just fold it up and put it back in your car. The paper bag—dependable, portable, within easy reach—the perfect container for a mouthful of rage.

If you see me by the side of the road, yelling into a paper bag, pull over and offer assistance. I'll be venting enough anger for two: me and my childhood self. I'm going to need two hands to hold the bag; will you tuck back my bologna curls for me while I scream?

CHAPTER 15
The Flight

Journal Entry: October 15

Coming up in a few weeks is my kayak trip to Mexico. I'll meet my friend Dora Jane in Los Angeles. My husband's not coming. I need to find out if I can take care of myself. This is a test.

Do I really want to let go of everything in the second half of my life—my house, furnishings, neighborhood, stability, steady income? Am I trying to run away from my responsibilities? Do I keep myself fat to keep me here? When I draw my problem with my husband and the scale is between us, in my mind the scale separates us. But now, it seems the polarity holds us together. All these years trying to fill up the hole inside with food when what I need is to love myself.

Yesterday when I was packing, I got the sense I was running away—almost a panicky feeling. Running away from the house made sense, but I have literally been running for the past few years. My sister Liz said, "What are you running from?" Running away from my husband, being responsible for him, feeling the pull to take care of him after his medical issues.

I know the only way I can work on myself is to get away. If I stay, I'll continue to be dependent and ignore all my own feelings and needs.

Now I'm leaving for my kayaking trip and when I come back, I'm leaving my husband of thirty-four years. Because I feel guilty and selfish, I rake the entire backyard before I go. I don't want him to think badly of me.

I decide to prepare for my trip to Mexico by learning to snorkel off our seawall here in the Keys. My trip isn't until the fall, so I figure this is a good time to learn. With limited experience, I ask an acquaintance to go with me. I put on a mask and snorkel and step into the Gulf of Mexico. Initially I have a hard time with my breathing. I'm hyperventilating at first and then the sight of the colorful fish soothe me and my breathing settles down.

I'm completely taken by the sea life when I see what looks like a huge boulder begin to move. I scramble to get to my feet, my arms flailing, pointing furiously. I can't get my voice. What is it? A shark, a whale?

As I start to scream "Help," someone yells out, "It's a manatee. I can see it's whiskers." I start to back up toward the shore, unsure of what to expect. People seem to come out of the cracks in the seawall. They're grabbing lettuce and apples. Someone gets a hose to give this sea cow water.

I'm in the perfect spot. I swim up to her and touch her skin, which is rough and ragged in places. This manatee has been damaged. She's been struck by propellers and other hazards on the sea of life. This day we swim together. I feed her apples. She shows me what it means to trust people—trust them to give her what she needs. I give her sustenance; she gives me hope.

Back home in Albany, my packing done, I'm in the shower and I notice something on my side, by my waist. It feels like a scab but I don't remember getting hurt. Yesterday I raked leaves in the backyard, but there was no impact with anything sharp. I need to get a magnifying mirror as it looks like what I thought was a scab is in fact moving—alive. When I get a close-up view, I can see the little legs. A tick. I've been bitten by a tick. I've taken many ticks off my dog Q so I know what to do—smother it first with oil or even peanut butter to kill it, then extract the tick, making sure to get all its body parts.

I know I'm supposed to take the tick to the Department of Health so they can determine the type of tick, then follow up with an appointment with my doctor. However, I'm flying out in the morning, staying at an airport hotel tonight where I use their "sleep, park, and fly" service. I don't have time to take care of this now. This avoidance of self-care is a pattern I struggle with all my life.

I wake up in the airport hotel with a wicked headache. Great, I get what feels like the beginning of a migraine and I'm not even out of bed. Downing three painkillers with caffeine does the trick and I catch the shuttle for the airport. In the terminal I spot one of those cinnamon bun places and I order the largest one they make. Slathering it with butter, I down it with more caffeine. My stomach starts to rumble in protest, but I overlook the warning signs and hustle to queue up for boarding. I'm in the A category so I quickly grab an aisle seat.

We are somewhere over Illinois when the headache comes back with a vengeance. And now I'm going to be sick. Quickly I run to the bathroom and lose everything in my stomach, sticky bun, coffee—everything. I can't raise my head from the commode. The flight attendant raps on the door,

"Are you ok in there."

Weakly I mumble, "I'm really sick."

Now I realize I'm taking way too much time in here. I clean up the best I can and, holding the wall, walk back to my seat in the cabin.

I'm now the "passenger from hell." Not only am I throwing up in the puke bag, I'm losing other fluids too. The flight attendant takes pity on me and hands me a big black bag.

"Those little things don't work very well when you're sick," he says. My humiliation is complete. No one will look me in the eye. I'm apologizing profusely but no one seems to hear me.

I should not have left on a trip after a tick bite. Who do I think I'm kidding taking off like this? This is what I get, thinking I can take care of myself, being selfish, wanting something just for me. I've made a mistake and this is just the beginning. If I could make myself a little smaller, I might be able to crawl under the seat and get lost. Then the captain announces our descent and I pray this is all over soon.

Bound for Burbank, we stop over in Las Vegas and I wait for everyone to get off the plane. I don't know whether to get up; I'm fearful what my seat cushion will reveal. Steeling myself, I depart the plane and head for the nearest lavatory. I remove my pants and underwear, tie my jacket around my waist and wash, rinse, and dry my soiled garments with the hand dryer. When I exit the bathroom, my clothes are damp but I think I'm presentable.

The last leg of my trip is both good and bad news—bad, I get my same seat—good, no one else has to sit on this squishy cushion. My seat mate, a good neighbor, leans over and asks if I feel better. I feel so bad that he has to sit next to me and my fluids. I say weakly, "I'm so sorry you have to sit next to me."

In his brightest and best voice, he chides, "Oh no, ma'am, your misfortune is my fortune. I was so thankful I wasn't the one who got sick that I played the slots in the terminal and won $1,500. You're my lady luck!"

Well doesn't that just beat all. There were slot machines in the airport. There were, however, no one-armed bandits in the ladies' room, but then I was a little distracted.

My sister Liz picks me up in Burbank and the car ride starts my stomach going all over again. When we get to her house, she gives me some ginger ale and puts me to bed. I sleep for what seems like two days and when I wake up, I feel wonderful. I have three days before I leave for Mexico so we are going to have some much-needed girl time.

When I tell Liz about the plane experience, she says, "Makes total sense to me, Kat. You needed to dump out, expunge, void all the negative energy you've been holding on to all these years. That was your body's way of preparing you for your new life. You had no control over any of it. Your body was in charge."

As we planned, I meet my kayaking buddy, Dora Jane, at LAX. This is to be our Baja trip together. I tell her that according to local lore, on this day, the Day of the Dead, *Dia de los Muertos*, the souls of ancestors come back from the dead in the form of monarch butterflies for their annual reunions. We're on the same path the monarchs take on their migration south.

As millions of butterflies converge in the forests in central Mexico, Dora Jane and I will touch down on a beach in La Paz for a kayak expedition into the Sea of Cortez. If any of my ancestors show up, they need to pass the kayak evacuation drill—where they tip the kayak over with you in it and you fight your way out of the cockpit—all this while underwater with a boat over your head.

I want Dora Jane to know where my mind is going to be during this maiden flight with my new and improved butterfly wings, so at lunch I confide I'm going back to the Keys alone. As the butterflies escape the harsh, cold winter up North, I'm leaving my marriage.

She is quiet for a minute then she says she has spent some time alone this summer so she understands exactly what I'm saying. I'm hesitant about sharing my plan with anyone, even Dora Jane, who tells me to call her DJ. Prior to this trip, when we discuss a joint excursion to Baja, I'm a little unsure. I'm leery about sharing an adventure with a bouffant-coifed blonde, embellished in jewels and outfitted in designer clothing.

Will she be able to live in a tent on the beach, this descendent of Southern aristocracy? She assures me she is well-steeped in experiences like dry camping, having raised three boys alone. As a single mom she has taken them on many trips with nothing but a tent and some sleeping bags. She proves to be as good as her word. When her Gucci bags never show up at the airport in La Paz, she borrows a pair of trunks from our guide. She wears those shorts for our entire Baja experience. Never once does she complain about no running water or creature comforts. We wash our hair in the sea with Joy dishwashing liquid and giggle the entire time.

Meanwhile our arrival in La Paz turns comical. DJ fills out all the papers on her missing luggage, including the designer label on her cases. Our travel company has assured us someone will meet us at the airport. We spot two fabulous-looking young men who escort us to the hotel. As we are babbling in the van, both high on life, I suddenly notice the sign on the dashboard.

"Are you, no, you are from Baja Experiences, right?"

They respond, "Oh, you girls are so funny, trying to make an American joke."

"Ummm, I'm not joking, guys, we are supposed to be with BE, not BKT—Baja Kayak Trips."

DJ's so busy chatting I'm not sure she even hears me. My heart starts hammering inside my chest. We are in a van, in Mexico, with two guys who are not who they are supposed to be. Yes, they're adorable, but I'm a practical sort of girl. I start asking questions:

"Who are you? Who do you work for? Do you have ID?"

And then they burst out laughing. I don't think this is funny at all. This is a foreign country. I've read about kidnappings. Now they wouldn't kidnap me, but Dora Jane, of Southern aristocracy, that's different. DJ has jewels and Gucci bags, but they couldn't know that. Right now she has no bags at all. And as to jewelry, these were our pre-trip instructions:

Please note: Do not wear any jewelry—not even rings. Sparkly rings can attract unwelcome attention when you are snorkeling. We want to avoid any encounters brought on by shiny jewels.

This is fine by me although I realize I might have trouble pulling off my wedding ring. In the past, dish detergent did the trick so I slather my ring finger and start wiggling the band. Maybe if I just leave it on for a while like you do with WD-40. Now that's a thought, some WD. Works for everything else. No deal, it doesn't budge. I have to cut it off—I'm talking about the ring.

Now it does seem a little impetuous since I've only just announced my desire for separation. But I'm a rules kinda gal—I do what I'm told. I'm going to have the platinum band I've worn for over thirty years removed from my hand by a jeweler. I'm pretty sure they do that sort of thing. And zip, zap, buzz and it's gone.

My red, puffy finger seems to be relieved; almost like it's been squeezed so tightly the circulation has been cut. Circulation, an interesting word; referring to the heart and all it holds. My ring finger is inflamed, another powerful word—derived from the word inflammation—swelling, edema, those telltale signs something is going wrong in my body. Time to send the healing cells to the wound and my immune system moves into action. This wound is both circulatory and inflammatory. Healing needs to take place. A sea kayaking trip might move the process forward.

Back in the getaway van with the kidnappers, it turns out our captors are none other than the frontmen of the competing tour company. We have both been foiled. They think we're really with their group and we're playing a practical joke. Funny Americans, you like to make jokes. We try to convince them we are with BE, not BKT. They make the call to headquarters and get the truth.

When they realize they've made a mistake, they shrug it off. No worries. They know Allesandro, our Baja guide, it's a small town, they add.

When we arrive at the hotel, our real guide is in the lobby. When he greets us I say, "Too bad you didn't meet us as planned. We just gave your tip to two guys from BKT. We thought they were you. They thought we were in their group. Worked out well for BKT."

Allesandro is not happy with my snide comment, but he is diplomatic, welcomes us to our hotel, and gives us our tour package. He tells us to have a good night's sleep and we are to meet on the beach across the street in the morning for our kayak exit drills. Tomorrow I will be sucking down seawater with that smart mouth of mine, ruing the day I ever spoke like that to the man who would have my life in his hands for the next seven days.

We assemble on the beach in La Paz and one by one we're tested on our ability to get out of the kayak in an emergency. We sit in the boat with our paddle as the guides turn the boat upside down. While underwater, we're to get out of the seat, turn the boat up, not lose our paddle, all the while holding our breath. As I wait my turn, I notice the lithe, svelte bodies of everyone in the group. The only other big person is our lead guide, Allesandro. I step forward and enter the cockpit. These are sea kayaks where you sit down into the boat, not what are known as sit-on-tops. Since this is the type of boat I have, I have no trouble getting in—well, I do have to tug at my thighs to get situated.

Before my brain can tell my hips this is a mistake, I'm turned upside down, suspended in the water, wedged into the shell, and my legs won't come free. The ultimate humiliation—I'm so fat I'm stuck in the boat—maybe I'll die right here—die of shame. If I had thought ahead, I could have rubbed on some suntan oil. Maybe extracting myself would have been easier with a coat of grease.

As I struggle to get free, I feel my panic begin to ebb. I've been here before, in this shell, this cocoon. I slow down my breathing, feel the molded plastic pinching my hips, and I ever so slightly push down against the seat with my left butt cheek and my right hip breaks free. As I come up to the surface, I gasp for air. I look at the relieved faces of my mates, those on this journey with me, and I read their eyes. My own eyes drop to the water, my chin on my chest, my shoulders slump.

I'm twelve and I'm trying to hide the bruises and welts. My shame is fully displayed in front of everyone now. I'm not going to be able to go on the expedition. I've failed the test. There's not a kayak in the world big enough to hold me. DJ puts her arms around me, and the tears start to form. Why does she comfort me? That just makes it worse. I'm not used to being comforted. I am not going to cry in front of everyone.

As I'm pulling up my cloak of dignity, Allesandro announces that I will accompany Pablo in one of the double kayaks. We are to anchor the trip. In the voice of an ambassador he adds, "I need two very strong paddlers to take the rear position on this journey. I'm asking Kat and Pablo to accept this assignment." Well, if you ask it like that, I accept.

For me, it will be a defining moment, as Pablo asks me to take the dominant position at the back of the boat. Pablo will turn out to be a renaissance man who speaks three languages, is trained as an architect, and is a gifted storyteller. Our days paddling will be magical.

Our expedition departs La Paz on a skiff. There are eight guests, two guides, and three men who cook, drive the boat, and make sure we have a wonderful experience. Their culinary skills on a beach with zero kitchen appliances are legendary. We consume a dishpan full of guacamole washed down with a five-gallon tub of margaritas. Cakes, tamales, burritos, ceviche from just-caught bonita are in their repertoire. Food is a highlight, but nothing overshadows the snorkeling adventure into the sea caves where we come face-to-face with the fearsome big males.

"Watch out for the big male sea lions," our guide warns. Have I just had some kind of flashback? Big males? Watch out? As the skiff slows, we are told to go below and put on our wet suits. Earlier I had chosen the XL size, hoping it would fit. Now as I'm struggling to get my legs in the bottoms, I realize I should have chosen the XXL. Too late. It's really hot down here and my heart is racing.

Before I came down here, I asked DJ, "You're not going to do this are you—get into that water?"

She looks at me fondly and says, as if speaking to a child, "Kat, that's why we're here."

Oh, got it. We're here to jump in this swirling sea, with creatures everywhere, and swim down into the caves with the big male sea lions. No way. I'm not going. Oh, ok, I'll go. But I don't want to.

After what seems like hours pulling and tugging at the latex, I get the suit on. When I come up the steps, I strut around, me in my wet suit, ready to meet the big males. Suddenly DJ starts laughing and I say, "What, is something wrong?"

"Your wet suit is on backward," she announces. Well, too bad for me, I'm going the way I am. Those males will never know the difference.

Poised on the side of the boat, I'm about to make a huge leap—into the dark green sea, into a place I have never been, into what can only be described as an unwelcoming environment.

"This is why I'm here…. This is why I'm here… This is why I'm here…" I chant under my breath and I close my eyes and give myself over to life. Not life as I know it, but a new life, a new spirit of curiosity and adventure. The big males are waiting below.

The guide takes my hand and together we enter the cave. Schools of sardine swarm around me and I'm mesmerized by their movement. I go back up for air and a tiny baby sea lion accompanies me, touching me, guiding me to the surface. Delirious, almost giddy, I want more, I want to see more. On my return I spot one of the big males. He has his eye on me. He's watching for the weak ones, the inexperienced, the timid who are his prey.

I glance around quickly, my eyes darting for our guide. I realize I'm giving myself away. The quick moves, the rapid heartbeat, the fog on my mask, all signs of my vulnerability—an invitation to the beast. As the big male starts toward me, I stop breathing; I am unable to move. With great determination I raise my arm, and from out of nowhere a hand grabs me and pulls me back to the surface, to safety.

Our guide has spotted my dilemma and rescues me. I need help to get back into the boat. My legs are limp noodles. I have to lie down; my limbs won't hold me up. Our guide reassures me it was not really a close call. "Those big guys just look mean, they wouldn't hurt you," he says confidently.

"Tell that to my heart," I whisper as I valiantly try to calm down my breathing.

I have other close calls in the days to come; some are with the sea water itself, others with sea creatures and aquatic life. Some close calls are of my own choosing. The ones I choose include big males with secrets.

CHAPTER 16
The Keys

Journal Entry: November 28

Now Q and I are headed to the Keys alone. My plan is to write while I'm there. I believe I can figure myself out if I have time to just focus on me. I seem to struggle with self-development and staying on my own path. I'd like to find meaning and purpose in my life. Would loving myself be enough of a goal?

Q and I leave for the Keys, just the two of us. We spend our days on the water, and while I'm writing, Q is learning how to chase fish in the shallows. One day, to my surprise, she catches one.

"Hey, did you see, did you see, she caught one, hey, is anyone watching?" But there is no one around so I keep writing in my journal. I actually enjoy our solitude. I don't want or need anyone.

Sure, I'd like to have a companion who dances. When we go down to the tiki and the band is playing, Captain Joe with the twinkling eyes seeks me out. He's a good dancer but he's not companion material—too much of a drinker—and then there's his wife.

I prefer to dance around the camper with Q. She's gotten pretty good. When I crank up Bob Seger's "Old Time Rock and Roll," she gets up on her back feet and puts her paws in my arms. It's quite a sight. She can easily take the place of any dancer guy I might want. At night though I've started hugging my pillow. Must be those hormones I'm taking.

This might not be the best place to meet someone, here in a campground in the Keys. I've seen some of the guys around here and all they do is fish and drink. And they're scraggly-looking, disheveled, and smelling of brine. Guys in a place like this are not going to be the permanent type. They live in homes that have wheels for a reason.

Yesterday one of our neighbors stopped by to see if I needed anything since I'm staying here by myself. Q got a little territorial and checked him out good before she let him on the site, but right away I could see he was really old and probably harmless.

"Just want you to know if there is anything you need, anything at all, I have all the tools."

Now I think this is a really nice offer but when I tell DJ she laughs and says, "Listen, Kat, he must be a hundred years old so tell him if his tools are the originals, you're not interested." Then we laugh all afternoon.

Q is kind of a celebrity here in the park and everyone likes her. She gets me invited to the best parties just by tugging at me and pulling me into the gathering.

"Hey," they say, "come and join us—we have lots of food and beer." There's always a treat for Q too—that's the plan.

Now the park owners are adding a dog park at the end of our street where Q can meet up and play with other dogs. My buddy Dora Jane has a German Shepherd named Whiskey, which she says is "a good name for a

Tennessee bitch." Then we both giggle like it's a joke but Q doesn't like big, scary dogs like shepherds. Now Coco, the little poodle, is more to Q's liking.

Most days Q sleeps on the cement pad, under the gumbo-limbo tree. She never wanders off, so I don't even tie her up. This morning, however, she seems agitated and unable to get comfortable. I go inside to tidy up the RV and leave her alone outside. When I go out to check on her, she's gone. Now I get frantic.

"Q, Q, where are you?"

Before I can get halfway down the street, my neighbor, who is sitting on his picnic table, yells, "I think Miss Q just took herself to the bathroom."

Isn't that just like Q. She's so well-trained she took herself to the dog park. They'll tell that story for years to come.

"Remember that yellow Lab who was so well trained she took herself to the dog park when she had to go? She must have had quite a pedigree."

CHAPTER 17
The Death

Journal Entry: November 30

    Dora Jane wants me to go to yoga class with her. Now I kayak and play tennis, but I'm not really up for any of this new age stuff. Plus, I'm big, not tiny like her, and I'm self-conscious about my weight. But she's persistent. When we get to class, the teacher, Bonnie, tells me yoga is not competitive and to only focus on myself, not look at the others and compare myself to them. Sure, that sounds good, but out of the corner of my eye I quietly gasp when they bend over and pull their arms up off their backs. I can barely clasp my hands together behind my back, never mind lifting them up.

    I don't think I can do yoga, but I'm determined not to let Dora Jane down. When Bonnie tells us at the end of the class to lie down on our mats and just let our bodies relax on the floor, this is my kind of yoga. She puts on some music to help us relax and just when I feel calm, I hear the beautiful voice of Shaina Noll singing, "How Could Anyone?" It's a haunting, mystical melody with lyrics that touch my soul.

Now I'm sobbing uncontrollably—tears I never shed when my marriage ended. Tears I've saved up my whole life. Tears for Kat, tears for my husband because I couldn't love him enough, tears for my children because my heart was covered in vines. And I wanted to know why? Why no one ever noticed. Why no one ever told me. Now I'm at yoga and maybe I'm not lithe and limber like the others, but I believe I have a beautiful soul. I memorize the words to the song, and I start to believe.

The call comes at twilight, that time of day when there's no light, no dark. "Kat, Mom is dying," whispers my brother Jerry.

I love the name Kat. Nowadays, most people call me Kate or Katherine. Only one boy ever called me Kat. Yes, Jerry, the handsome man. As I unpack the paper bags, I can see him smile when he leans in, touches my cheek, and calls me Kat. I wonder if it's too late…. No, I think I heard he died, lung cancer. A big smoker and drinker, his ancestry was German, but he could've easily been Irish.

My mother's timing is a little off on this dying thing. Wildfires are burning in the Florida Keys and the main road, US 1, is closed. The only other possible way to exit the island is Card Sound Road, which is shrouded in smoke and impassable tonight. The Monroe County Sheriff's Department has issued a statement: "We believe citizens will be able to leave Key Largo on Card Sound Road in the morning." I would be first in line.

My concern with the smoke is my Q, my companion, my beautiful Lab. I can put a wet washcloth over my nose and mouth, but she has no protection from the white stuff as it billows through the engine and up into the car. It's not like I can speed up. Visibility is nil. There's no turning back, I'm committed to seeing this death watch through. How ironic I would take this kind of heroic gesture in order to be with my mother when she dies.

The journey takes two days. Toward the end, on a lonely dark road in central Pennsylvania, I start to realize there's no way I can do this. I cannot care for my mother as she dies. My feelings for my mother are ambivalent. How do I show her the love she never showed me? Thoughts are jumbled in my head, paper bags full of memories, I remember …. Crash, something strikes the hood of my car, dear God in heaven, something is leaping over the front of the car. I think it's an elk. Whatever it is, it's huge, barely grazes the windshield and, whoosh, it's gone. There's no place to pull over on the dark and winding road and the realization hits me, I'm in Elk County, Pennsylvania.

When I'm able to pull safely off the road, my knees shaking so badly I can barely get out of the car, I get my flashlight to inspect the damage. What I find embedded in the grill of the car are clumps of hair, wisps of white and gray. There's no damage to me or my car. What the elk has left are the tufts of a brush with death. My own. I've been spared. You don't walk away from a collision with an elk.

This is what it takes to get my attention. An elk. On a dark, lonely road in the middle of nowhere. This road, another time, we would be racing the curves, defying death, in my brother's jalopy. Now I'm heading to a different death, and I'm not ready for this one. As I pull into Our Jerry's house, it's all lit up, there seem to be a lot of cars. The back room has been set up with a hospital bed and there in the dimmest light is my mother.

As my eyes adjust to the darkness, I can see someone is feeding her and touching her lovingly. Getting closer, I smile a knowing smile. It's my daughter, one of my mother's favorite grands. In that glimpse of love I realize I can do it. This is my daughter who is caring for her grandmother. She must have driven all the way from Philadelphia after work to be here. This is the child I raised. If she can bathe my mother's face, caress her, and let her know how much she's loved, I can help my mother die.

Now this dying takes on epic proportions. It will take four months for me to understand it as honoring; showing the matriarch her life is valued while she is still alive. Her wish is to have all the nieces, nephews, and cousins visit while she still has a breath. As luck or hard work would have it, Our Jerry owns a hotel in town. And a pharmacy, a restaurant, a camp in the woods, and an old garage where he stores his vintage automobiles. He's the proverbial big fish. Sandy, his second wife, makes it all happen. She's the daughter I aspire to be. I watch her, how she coddles my mother, bathing her, caring for her with love. I'm not sure I can do it, but with Sandy as my model, I accept the challenge.

With Our Jerry and Sandy as hosts, we bring in the family: McNeils from New Jersey, Ruddys from Albany, McDonalds from Scranton, McHughs from Reading, and on it goes. Each and every one makes the trek up US 6, a throwback in time, a road untouched, bringing their stories of the good old days. Their parents, gone now; my mother is the last of her siblings alive. She's been the clarion of the family, the one who made the calls of congratulations, announcements, good news and bad. The glue that held them all together.

When we gather, everyone knows a story about Mom and her eccentricities, as all the cousins fondly call them. Known as Milly or Mil, short for Mildred, my mother's "Millyisms" would be her legacy. To this day family members revel in the stories about my mother and her lack of tact and diplomacy. How daughters-in-law would be horrified and angered by my mother's harsh scrutinizing of her grandchildren for defects: "Does his eye always have that weird look to it? Maybe he has a lazy eye like Our Jerry."

These criticisms taken to heart by some as ill will or downright meanness were just shrugged off by the five of us, her children. We grew up with a mouth that had no filter. We knew how cruel she could be. When Liz got divorced, Mom kept harping on and on about the fact that Liz's children were in the custody of her ex-husband.

"What kind of mother would give up her children?" Mom would rant.

I got tired of hearing it and in one of my harsher moments with my mother, I spewed out, "Mom, if you and Dad had gotten divorced, and we each had a choice, you or Dad, where do you think we would have gone?" And, just to make sure she got it, "We would all have gone with Dad. You would have been a woman who gave up her children."

Whether my mother understood what I said or not, it got her attention as she sputtered and mumbled and did that twitching thing she always did with her hands. I just couldn't stand her putting down my sister Liz in this way. I can be cruel too.

When we were growing up, anger would spew from Mom's mouth and all of us, especially my dad, were fair game.

"You're not using your brilliant mind," she would harp. "You could be anything you want."

My mother's disdain for my father's lack of "get up and go" would eventually wear him down. What my dad wanted was to escape. He built a horseshoe pit behind our house as a sanctuary. We would hear the clinks and clangs as he heaved those shoes until he wore himself out. Then he would come in, go to their bedroom, and get down on his knees and pray. He never told us his prayers but even as kids we knew what he prayed for. They had five kids and no money. My mother used to say about my dad, "He'll never set the world on fire." My parents never fought, or I should say, my father never fought back.

I learned the art of nonconfrontation at the knee of my father. Passive-aggressive, my dad would mock my mother behind her back. The boys thought it was funny. I hated it. The mocking set the scene for the beatings to follow. I thought I hated my father, but I would become just like him. When our marriage counselor would ask me to describe my role models for love, I would hesitate and start to unpack the emotions. What a curious question. Who is your role model for love?

I was in trouble. Peace at all cost. But the cost had been my life. I could barely think for myself. When I told my mother I was getting a divorce, she asked, "Why can't you just stay in the same house, there are two floors. You can be on one floor and he can be on the other."

Bingo! That is what she had done. They led separate lives. My husband and I had lived in a similar way. I did my thing, he did his. I turned our union into my parents' marriage.

As April turns into June, my mother holds on. Each night as she goes to bed she warns us, "This is the night. I'll be dead in the morning."

My brother Eddie is here for the weekend and as the four of us are sitting around the kitchen table, in strolls our mother. Sandy and Jerry look up and Mom says, "I'm hungry. I think I'll make a peanut butter sandwich."

With my smart mouth, I say, "Gee, Mom, I thought this was going to be the night."

Not missing a beat, Eddie adds, "Yeah, Mom, what are you going to do, take it with you?"

Sharply turning on her heel, she gives us the evil eye and shuffles back to bed. We burst out laughing, a tension-reliever if I've ever lived one. This honoring your mother stuff is exhausting.

The next morning the visiting nurse stops by.

"Mildred," she says, "We need to talk about your impending death."

My mother has congestive heart failure and is on oxygen all the time now. She's getting frailer by the day. Her mind, however, is as sharp as ever. In her best Milly voice, my mother snaps, "I know exactly when I'm going to die."

"Is that right," says the nurse. "When is that?"

Drawing in a big breath, my mother quips, "I'm going to die when my Katherine leaves me."

The nurse turns to me, confusion on her face and I say, "See these shoulders, Mom, I can take it. Put it right here where it belongs."

As it turns out that is exactly what happens. I leave in July for a one-week consulting job at Colgate University where I facilitate the weeklong workshops Phyllis Brown foretells will bring the teachers into the era of standards. I act as the assessor determining whether educators are learning what they need as these changes take place in each of their school districts.

Phil would be a prophet, and as she predicted, our work would produce school principals, curriculum directors, even school superintendents steeped in and grounded in a background of nurturing the whole child. We'd be thwarted, however, in the very place that should have been the bastion of nurturance, the department of education. After a weeklong training session, I'm giving my report on teachers' readiness to change, a pre- and post-evaluation with data on the results, when the room gets quiet.

One honcho, a top administrator, says, "We're not interested in this gooey stuff, these soft skills, we want to know what they learned? Did they learn math? Did they learn spelling? We don't want to hear all this nurturing talk."

One of our college professors can't contain herself, she blurts out, "Let me get this straight. You're not interested in nurture, the very heart of our profession?"

The room gets deathly still, and the top administrator says, "That's not what we said. Not what we meant. You've gotten us off track. Just leave your papers and data. This meeting is over."

My days of assessing teachers would also be over. No wonder morale was so low. There was no way I could go into those summer institutes and measure how much content the teachers were learning. I wanted to know if they could accept the changes brought about by the new movement to standards, and if they could change, what those changes would look like in their classroom, and then how those changes would affect their students.

With all this focus on change, I could no longer go on as always. I was becoming a leader, I felt valued and I was compensated for my expertise. Not only was I proposing teachers change but through this process, I personally would change. The consulting money I make gives me the confidence and financial independence to be able to say, "I can take care of myself."

I find the courage to tell my husband I want a divorce. When I look back, I realize I could never have done this without the support of my mentor and friend Phil. She believed in me and together we created a team of teachers who would be critical in moving FCS to the twenty-first century.

All the friendships and camaraderie we experienced as a team in this effort to move forward are still strong today. The standout teachers have become thought leaders who will not be stopped and will keep the nurturance of children alive in their districts. Phil will retire from her job at the department, but we all know what we accomplished and have a sense of pride as we look back.

Phil and I are friends always. I'll never forget the faith she had in me and my big ideas—ideas that matched her very own. Together we are a formidable force and I treasure the memories of the years when, just as Phil predicted, we laid the tracks for the future of family and consumer sciences.

My mother dies as she predicted: on her own terms in her own time. I'm gone one day, on my way to Hamilton, New York, and she pulls the plug. When Our Jerry calls me, his voice cracking, he says, "The nurses found her in her chair. She pulled out her oxygen cord." My mother always called the shots right to the very end.

PART II
ADDICTIONS

CHAPTER 18
Omissions

Journal Entry: February 7

I've been given the gift of love. Incredible as it is, this love is cloaked in omissions and avoidance of truth. Not outright lies, these are what I call "omissions"—things never mentioned, overlooked—briefly covered by words like "I have issues."

This phrase works well for someone like me who never confronts because, basically, I don't want to know the truth—can't handle the truth—never even ask what these issues are.

I'm so desperate to be loved, I can't even call them what they are—I call them omissions.

Sal and I have campers in the Keys, in Marathon, a drinking town with a big fishing problem, or maybe it's a fishing town with a big drinking problem. People are here to party. There's a lot of drinking that goes on.

Most are here for the beautiful water. On one side of the chain of islands you have the Atlantic Ocean, on the other the Gulf of Mexico. Take your pick they are both breathtaking in their beauty.

Lots of people fish here. I kayak. Kayaking is the perfect sport for me—peaceful, quiet, almost meditative. I can drop my boat over the sea wall and in two minutes I'm in the water. The water is crystal clear, and you can see all the way to the sandy bottom. It's easy to glimpse dolphin, shark, and lovely spotted rays as they glide gracefully across the sea floor. My friends and I kayak every day.

I want to take Sal for a sunset paddle on his day off, to give him an idea just how spectacular it is to skim across the water as the sky lights up with purples and pinks. We borrow my friend DJ's kayak for his maiden voyage. I suggest he might want to bring some beer as we will be out there for at least an hour. His response stuns me.

"No beer. I want to be fully present for this incredible voyage. I don't want anything to take away from this night."

I hear him say, "fully present, don't want anything to take away." Is that what the beer does? Does it take him away? From real life? From me? As we head out into the sunset, I file this away. No, I don't ask what he means. I never ask. When we get back from our ride, the cooler comes out and consumption begins.

Next week is Valentine's Day. It will be our first. We plan to celebrate in a big way with gifts and food; he'll cook for me. The night before the big day, as he leaves to go back to his trailer, having consumed a few beers, he tells me he'll be over later in the morning, before noon. This is exciting, as I never see him in the morning before he goes to work We agree on the time.

In the morning, I start to prep the trailer. I have candles everywhere. I bring out all the big guns: chocolate, almonds, even figs. I've draped the bed in lovely silk sheets. At 11:50 a.m., I light all the candles. The entire fifth wheel is glowing. I'm starting to quiver in anticipation.

At 1:15 p.m., the candles start to flicker out and I realize he's not coming. He doesn't have a phone so I can't call him, and I probably wouldn't do that anyway. I can't stop the tears as they start to fall from my eyes and across my chin. I've been stood up. What a fool. To think he would choose me, this lovely boy. As I move through my home, putting out the candles that are still left, I start to get really angry.

How dare he stand me up? As I'm starting to get worked up, there is a knock at the door. And there he is with a gift and a grin. I've already taken off my seduction clothes and washed my face. Eyes swollen, gritting my teeth, I turn on him with vengeance.

"We had a date for noon—you said you'd be over by noon. Now it's almost 1:30," and vitriol spews out of my mouth. "I don't have to…"

He interrupts my harangue with a curt voice, "Looks like we've gotten off to a bad start here. I'll be back in an hour and we'll see if we can start this date over." With that he turns and walks away down the street.

I go inside and start to throw everything I can get my hands on. Who does he think he is? Now I'm a full-blown lunatic. Nobody will treat me like this. I scream, rant, and then I can't even catch my breath I'm sobbing so hard. It's, it's … can't get air, can't suck in any air. I'm gasping for air. Maybe I'm having a heart attack. Yes, that's it. It definitely has something to do with my heart.

I have no experience whatsoever with any kind of crying. I never cry. I can't seem to stop. My practical mind is repulsed. "Get ahold of yourself, girl." I'm always under control, tightly wound. But, I've become unglued; lost all touch with reality. Did he say one hour? He'll be back in one hour? Do I still have a few minutes before he comes back?

With only seconds to spare, I wipe my face and fluff up my hair as he knocks and enters my home for the second time today. He's smiling that knowing smile. I start to tell him how many candles I had lit and how pretty the room… I can't finish because he's taken me into his arms and is kissing my wet cheeks and my tear-swollen eyes.

I never let on what I start to understand—he drank so much last night, he didn't even remember what he said. But why did he bother to give me a time? Why tell me the night before he's coming over in the morning? Why not just say, "I'll see you at 1:30"?

Isn't that the big question? I will begin to learn this is the disease—the promises, good intentions, the list of things he's going to do—tomorrow. All promised the night before under the influence of booze.

My hugger/dancer Sal and I have decided to travel north together and stay in his camper on the trip. It will be our first time living together. We're part of the migration—the snowbirds that fly south in the winter. It's now April and we reverse our course. We drive in separate cars as I'm meeting a work friend in Roanoke. Our plan is to split up in Richmond, going our separate ways.

We stop at Green Acres RV Park with the longest pull-through sites on I-95. Pull-through sites are premium. You don't unhook your truck when you pull in, and the next morning you drive straight out. Never once do you have to back up or unhitch the trailer. We are happy campers. Dinner is to be a roast chicken with all the fixings. I don't lift a finger. I'm being waited on, catered to, maybe even cherished.

When it's time to eat, I start to sit and I notice the table is set for one. What's going on here?

"Aren't you eating? If you don't want to eat now, I'll just wait for you." This is really weird. Why go to all this trouble and then not eat? I've got a million questions. I don't get it; I don't have a clue what is going on here.

My hands start to twitch; oh God, like my mom's do when she gets anxious. I get up from the table to start to leave when two hands on my shoulders stop me. Turning me around to face him, he asks me to look at him. I don't want to, don't want to hear what he's going to say.

"Look at me," he pleads. "You need to know this. I'm an alcoholic. I don't eat when I have a buzz. Food will take away from the effect. I want you to eat now, I'll eat something later." And because I do what I'm asked, I sit down but I just pick at the food—this feast that has been prepared so lovingly. I have a huge lump in my throat, but I force myself to eat a little something. When I'm finished, I get up from the table and say good night. He works on his buzz.

I get into bed, but I don't cry. An alcoholic; he's an alcoholic. Once said it cannot be taken back. I can't pretend any longer. He had to hold me by the shoulders, look me in the eye, even ask me to make eye contact, which I didn't want to do, because I knew deep down what was coming. "I'm an alcoholic."

All these months with the ever-ready cooler and I refused to accept it, looked the other way, convinced myself it was just a little beer. Resolute, I plan my getaway. There are two vehicles. I'll head to Roanoke and we'll be done, over, caput. I won't think about all the signs I should have noticed: the continual trips to the refrigerator, the asking me to drive on our first date. What a stupid girl. Sure, he drinks a lot but it's only beer. Did I mention he smokes also? Here, in the trailer, while I sleep in the back. Another omission on my part. I never ask him to smoke outside. It's his trailer after all.

I'll leave in the morning before he wakes up. Turning, twisting, fidgeting, I can't find sleep. As dawn starts to break, I make my move. It's awkward because I'm against the wall. I will have to crawl over him. With one leg over his body, I see him startle and come fully awake.

"I'm leaving you," I declare. "I can't do this."

His face breaks into pieces: eyes first, then lips, his chin drops, "Don't do this, don't go." I lumber over him and barely make it to the bathroom before I throw up. I can't lift my head from the toilet. Dizzy, my heart pounding, I'm seriously ill. I can't stop vomiting.

Then it hits me, the realization. I can't leave. My mind says yes, but my body has a different plan. I guess my heart is part of my body, even though I've always kept it pretty well walled off. There's no connection here to my brain. I know what I should do but that's not what I'm going to do. I get back in bed, feel his arms around me, spooning me, holding me close, telling me to never let him go. That's what my heart and my body want. My brain takes a backseat.

We're watching a movie and Sal gets up to get a beer eight or ten times in those few hours. My only memory of this pattern is when I would stop and visit my brother Joey. As I'm traveling around New York doing my consulting work, Joey's house was my hitching post. I'd pull in and visit and then stay overnight. We'd hang out, watch tv, chat, and his wife Sue and I would have a glass of wine.

I remember Joey would get up and go to the kitchen for an O'Doul's seven or eight times in an evening. Now I realize this is a nonalcoholic beverage, but I have nothing else to link this behavior to. Yes, it's obsessive but is it an addiction?

Peeking in my paper bags, with a sense of wonder, I begin to see how I justify Sal's drinking. I start by ruminating, turning it over and over in my mind, looking for a way to condone it. Then I hit on someone I love who showed a similar inclination—my brother Joey.

Even though Joey's drink was not alcohol, the incessant round-trip to the refrigerator feels exactly the same, same urgency, same laser focus. So, Sal has what looks like the same affliction as my brother Joey, and while this doesn't portend well, I make it one of my own omissions—I refuse to accept what is right in front of my face—all the while knowing it's the harbinger of death.

CHAPTER 19
Acceptance

Journal Entry: March 4

How would my life look if I focused on addiction and made it my life's purpose? My own addiction is to food and pleasing others. What I do is figure out what you want to hear and then I say it or do it. Where does authenticity fit in with this addiction? Are they tied together or diametrically opposed?

My guess is addiction keeps me from being authentic. Pain and guilt are trapped in the addiction—they mask it and keep the brain anesthetized from feeling. Authenticity would accept the pain and guilt and invite it to come forth. In my case, the addiction keeps me from fulfilling my potential. I have talent but I keep it hidden under a layer of armor that resembles fat. When I put on the armor, I can spend my energy berating myself for eating too much and then my focus is on my body image and I'm right back to pain and guilt.

How would authenticity combat that cycle? Would it keep me from eating when I'm not hungry? If the pain and guilt are the underlying emotions, then the authenticity needs to fight that battle. How can authenticity fight pain and guilt?

It has to be more than just speaking up. It has to be related to the cause of the pain and guilt and I'm right back to the addiction. I can see how much I'm in my head—how much time I spend ruminating and analyzing myself. I'm hoping I can learn to live with the addictions as I work toward a healthier lifestyle.

"God, grant me the serenity to accept…" I'm new at this acceptance stuff. All around me are a million things, people, situations I need to accept.

"Um, excuse me. I don't have the problem, someone else has the problem. You mean I have to come here and learn all of this? But it's not me who has the problem." I cross my arms and start to mumble, "This isn't fair. It's not me. I'm not the one…" Now I start to tsk tsk tsk and roll my eyes.

I'm going to ditch this place with all these weird rules and ridiculous steps. These people are so strange they're even chanting. And all these affirmations and plaudits. My jaw tightens, and I can feel a full-blown hissy fit begin to form. Clinching my teeth so hard I think I hear one of my crowns break, I steel myself. Dear God, this is not what I meant when I asked for your help.

Looking for guidance on how to live this life, I happen on a book called the *I-Ching—The Book of Changes.* This is an ancient Chinese divination text offering guidance for moral decision making. It's a much more forgiving guide than this den of religious fanatics I've stumbled on. I can find clarity just by throwing three coins; I use shiny copper pennies.

My hexagram tells me to retreat. The Chinese character is a pig running away so as not to be eaten. Now this is more like it. Not only do I get direction, I get a visual—a pig. What I do know about myself is this is how I learn. I have no one I can talk to about this. My sister Liz told me to see those serenity people, so I went. "But, Liz, they want me to accept that I have a problem, which I clearly don't."

139

"Oh, you have a problem," the weirdos repeat. I think there is something seriously wrong with one of us here. There are eight or nine people sitting around this table and they all agree.

"But I'm not the alcoholic," I recite. "I have no idea why my sister told me to come here."

I remember this morning's I-Ching reading: *The hermit, faithful to the truth he believes, escapes from community into himself.* Sometimes I have a hard time translating the words but this one is easy. I'm the hermit.

But there is another piece to the hexagram—*the truth*. What is the truth? Why am I so angry at the churchy people? To be this entrenched and stubborn there must be some truth I'm trying to hide, something I don't want to accept.

The *I-Ching* warns: *When you hide away, you could lose yourself.* I will do what I need to do to stay safe and whole. I keep coming to these meetings and I start to understand the truth. I have a problem. I love an alcoholic.

File it under Omission, an avoidance of truth. I was asked to be the driver on our first date. At the time I thought it peculiar. In fact, I wondered if I should have been more curious? Nevertheless, I will treat it as a minor detail, certainly nothing to fuss about or ponder. Come on, it's only beer, never the hard stuff. Just goes to show you how much of a problem I have. Omissions will start to stack up in our relationship. I will be undaunted. I was married for thirty-four years before I was able to say, "Whoa, stop!" I don't do confrontation.

Sal and I are heading back to the Keys for the winter. We will each have our own RVs when we get there, but we will make the eleven-hundred-mile trip together—as in cohabitation. I'm in the bedroom finishing my packing as he comes in my daughter's front door to pick me up for the trip. He says to my daughter and her husband, "I want to reassure you that I will take good care of your mother. I will not let anything happen to her."

How lovely to overhear this thoughtful message to my daughter, "Your mom is safe with me." I admit it doesn't take much kindness to get to me, but this conversation I put into his bank account of love. This account has nothing to do with finances. I start to fill up this account with his acts of loving kindness, like how he opens the car door for me and then turns and helps Q get into the backseat, or how he cooks for me and caters to my every need.

As this loving account starts to accumulate, I begin to feel cherished and all my worries about what's right, what people think, even what my kids say, no longer have importance. My own compass is my guide. I overlook omissions, part-truths, and promises made after many beers. The love account overflows; I'm completely smitten, and fall deeply in love.

The glorious food Sal prepares for me on the beach is legendary. He brings a Coleman stove with him in the truck and proceeds to set it up and cook gourmet meals right there in the sand. He has brought everything he needs to make me scallops primavera and oysters Rockefeller and I'm in heaven. Yes, this is how you woo me: kindness, thoughtfulness, and maybe a side of shrimp scampi.

There are, however, other omissions—financial instability, a school loan never paid, and other bigger secrets that come out eventually. There is one omission that cannot be covered up—anger. He is quick to anger and it includes expletives and throwing things.

We are in the car heading to the beach when all of a sudden he slams his fist against the dashboard. "Jesus Christ, I can't believe I left it! Damn it! Fuck, fuck, fuck!" He keeps slamming his hand again and again. Then he grabs his mug and throws it into the backseat.

I'm holding my breath and I begin to cower against the car door. I don't even ask what's going on. Now he makes a U-turn and we're heading back to the camper way too fast. Fear is pulling at me and I try to get really small, invisible. When we get back, he slams the car door so hard I think I hear the glass shatter. He goes into the camper and comes out with a package of meat. This tantrum was about forgetting to put the meat in the cooler.

I'm very quiet, I hardly breathe, never say a word. I've been here a million times and I never make the mistake of correcting or commenting. I just curl up and go deep inside. I look for the blue satin quilt but it's nowhere to be found. What were the chances that as lovely as he is, he would also be an angry man?

I'm beginning to understand one of my life lessons is to figure out how not to let the anger make me feel small and helpless. I see the pattern, the event that causes it, the way my body responds, where I go in my mind, yet I struggle with those beliefs about myself that keep me trapped in this dynamic—the unworthiness and shame.

I'm big on making excuses for all of Sal's behavior, including the anger. Along with the anger is a penchant for wandering, as glimpsed in his favorite movie with the theme song "Wand'rin Star." When things and people get to be too much, it's time for the star, Lee Marvin, to hit the road and head west and the life of a loner.

Sal tells me after his divorce, he perfected his *Paint Your Wagon* persona, not wanting or needing anyone in his life. This estrangement led to living and working in New Mexico for years. Then a family medical emergency called him back to the east and through some twist of fate, he ended up in a campground in Marathon, Florida in the Keys. On a beautiful evening in November, he put on his bathing suit and headed down to the water for a swim and a few dives before the sun went down.

PART III

THE HUGGER/DANCER

CHAPTER 20
The Dump

Journal Entry: August 1

I'm waiting for his call. It's his day off—we should be together, but we won't be because this coming and going is not working for him. I think he'd rather live in his memory than commit to a future with me. So now I'm actually considering only seeing him in the Keys, like I can be put on a shelf and brought out during winter season. Like I'll take anything I can get.

That puts me right back in the vicious cycle of giving, giving, giving. How do I get out of it? This is my chance, right here, right now. If/when he calls, I have to let him know that will not work for me—I will not be put on a shelf to be opened at Christmas. I can't love him four to five months of the year and that's it. Can I be resolved with this?

As I'm waiting, I decide I can send him a card at the campground where he is staying. I find a simple card with a sailboat on the front. The sailboat is a reference to the Valentine's Day gift he bought for us—a huge rock with a boat clinging to it. He likened it to our relationship—a port in a storm. It's a lovely unique gift.

My love, this card reminded me of the sailboat on our rock.
I want you to know you've given me the ultimate gift—
you've helped me to see that I am capable of loving (you)
at a level I never thought possible. I'm trying to accept
that things are as they need to be for reasons that I cannot understand.
I love you.

Journal Entry: August 9

After spending the day yesterday with Phyllis and Sheila at the pool, I've decided to go after the man I love. I'm not sure I have the courage, if that's what this takes. Maybe I'm going to get hurt but I truly believe Sal loves me.

Q comes with me because she's a companion that never judges me or narrows her eyes or even snarls. She just wants to be with me. I put her in the car hours before I'm ready to leave to reassure her she won't be left behind. We have that certain insecurity in common.

No longer dancing, no more rapture, we have migrated north for the summer season, me to my four-bedroom house and my hugger/dancer to his wandering lifestyle. I'm pacing around the kitchen waiting for the phone to ring. Anxious and waiting, it's what I do. When your lover is footloose and a rambler, with no cell phone, you wait—wait for him to call, wait for him to choose.

The phone finally rings, and I can barely speak. I start to babble on about coming to see him and suddenly the phone is quiet like there's no one there. In a whisper he says, "You can't come up this weekend."

"OK," I say, "I'll come up next weekend."

"No," he says, "I can't commit to you and our relationship—it's not working for me. I do love you, but this is not about you—this is about me and my lifestyle. I'll see you in the Keys. Maybe we can see each other during the winter season." Then he tells me he'll call later next week.

I stammer, "Don't you want to see me?" There is no more communication—he hangs up.

Oh God, I'm being dumped. I stand there and look at the phone like it's a foreign object. Then something breaks inside me and I start to do something I have never done in my entire life: I rail and scream and slam my fists against the wall. I try to calm down in the basement with yoga, but I end up pounding my fists into the floor as I sob uncontrollably. It can't end like this. I know he loves me.

I've been following him around all summer. Staying here and there while literally chasing him. I show up unexpectedly at his trailer and he's clearly not happy to see me. Plans? No problem, I can wait.

The next day he says, "You and Q will have to leave—I'm going to Philly for a job." I'm bereft, when will we see each other? Can I come? I'm pathetic. I've reached even lower than those paper bags in the backseat of my car. Then he tells me he'll call me once he gets established with his job.

I throw back my shoulders and pull myself together. I play his favorite music and cry. I don't understand what I've done, how I could have lost his love. I'm analyzing every word of my last conversation with him. Mostly I'm trying to figure myself out. Is all this pain coming from my attempts to let him go, a kind of grieving, or is it me wanting to be attached and refusing to accept the fact we're done?

I understand the shock of it, being blindsided, but I'm starting to wonder who I was fooling when I said I didn't want to make a commitment after being married for thirty-four years. And then the obvious hits me— I've lied to myself about not wanting to commit to him because I knew he was unavailable. I figured if I told him what I needed it would scare him away and so I tried to be what he wanted. And here I am again letting my needs take a backseat—back there with my paper bags.

I can't call him. I can only wait for him to call me. Since the dump I haven't heard a word. I know he loves me. I couldn't be wrong about that. It does occur to me that he is unavailable, not interested in staying in one place with one person, but I dismiss these thoughts immediately. I see him hitching up his wagon, getting away from me as fast as he can. I've tried not to hold on too tightly, but my love is all-consuming. I don't think I could have done anything differently, and now I have to live with the consequences of opening myself to love and being vulnerable. It's not like I never had clues about his rambling ways.

I remember the night he brought out his favorite movie, *Paint Your Wagon*. Our hero is the love 'em and leave 'em classic kind of guy. Just to make sure I'm paying attention, he says, "That's me and my lifestyle—just the way I like it." Well, I think to myself, that's about to change.

I've been dumped, and Q and I are driving to meet with Sheila, the craniosacral therapist, to find out how I can deal with this loss. I'm hoping her head and neck massage helps me to try to understand why I've lost the love of my life—my hugger/dancer. I'm a masochist, my Neil Young disc is playing in the background. I try to keep my watery eyes on the highway.

We meet and I explain to Sheila my predicament.

"Sheila, I want to dance again, to feel the rapture. I'm afraid I will never feel it again." Now I'm whining.

"I can give you my craniosacral touch," she explains, "but it won't bring you what you desire. I can help you reach those feelings buried deep inside and I can make you cry."

Jeez, I think, that is not something I need help with anymore. I cry all the time these days. But those feelings, what about those feelings? My unworthiness, the shame, and its twin the perfectionism, that might be a good place to start. My friends will become the critical piece in our lives, but then they've been to Lilydale too, and maybe they already know my future.

I'm at the pool with Phyllis and Sheila, and I keep getting up and checking my phone.

"What the heck are you doing?" they ask.

"I'm waiting for him to call me," I say.

"Well, you can't sit around all day waiting for him to call you, you have to go see him, insert yourself into his life, be in his face, find out whether he loves you or not," they scold. "Why wait," they say. "Go up there and ask him face-to-face what's going on."

"Oh," I say, "I could never do that; that would be pushy, aggressive. He won't like that. I'll wait till he calls me." Now that's me of the wait-and-see attitude, certainly not the school of confrontation.

My reticence only makes them more adamant. Just to shut them up, I agree. I'm working tomorrow so it will have to wait. They know me and my avoidance of conflict: peace at all cost. They tell me they'll be driving up there themselves if I don't come through. And I know they will do exactly that. I like the way my friends insert themselves into my life; it feels like love to me, like being taken care of and loved.

Q and I arrive at the campground and there's no one around, no truck, nothing. It's pitch black in the woods and it's still raining. Q is lying in the backseat, and everything is still; all you hear is the rain on the roof of the car. We've been in the car for a long time on this trip up here, long enough for me to understand what I've become—a love-starved stalker. Always so perfect in every way, now with my inhibitions gone, I make no pretense of respectability; it's like I have nothing left to lose.

The truth is we've been following Sal around all summer, chasing him. We show up unexpectedly at his trailer, but he has plans.

"No problem, we can wait." The next day he tells us we have to leave. Now I'm even whining, "When will we see each other? Can I come?"

I'm pathetic. I wonder if the fact that he doesn't like dogs has anything to do with his pushing us away. He tolerates Q but then_she's a pretty amazing beast.

The guy is unavailable, not available for love, not capable of domestication. For someone who's supposed to be smart, I just don't understand. Maybe I just want the challenge—to get the unavailable boy? Would getting Sal make me feel worthy of love? This guy? This drinker who calls himself a bum? He of the "what you see is what you get" philosophy? Why doesn't all that talk scare me away?

As I lie in wait in the car, there's the scent of danger. What's the matter with me? I need to get out of here right now. Just as I start to turn on the ignition, his headlights round the corner. What must he think? He comes to the car, I roll down the window and say the dumbest thing I've ever spoken in my life: "I'm not stalking you."

Sal thinks this is funny and he smiles. "What are you doing here?" he asks.

I mumble something about coming up to get at the truth.

"Wait here," he says in a voice that sounds like a command. He turns his back and walks into the trailer.

Q and I have made the trip to Sal's camper and we're sitting out here in the car in the middle of a rainstorm waiting. What are we waiting for? Sal asked us to stay in the car, but that must have been ten or fifteen minutes ago. Does he need to tidy up the camper before inviting us in?

I have no idea what is taking so long but I'm starting to regret the decision to come up here, to chase after him. I own a house in suburbia and a camper in the Keys, but I pine for a thirty-foot trailer in the middle of the woods with my hugger/dancer. I am out of my mind.

After what seems like an eternity Sal returns and brings me to sit on a chair under the awning of the trailer. He's not even inviting me inside. He positions his chair directly across from mine. We are face-to-face. There's no touching.

His opening line I will never forget:

"You deserve to know the truth, why I asked you to stop coming up here. There's something I never told you about me. I like to dress in women's clothes. It's something I do almost every morning. I do love you, but my lifestyle will always come before anyone or anything. I will not be a case study, project, or anyone's property. There are different names for what I do; if you want to learn more, you can search the internet.

At first, I think he's kidding but I quickly realize he's serious. My eyes start to blink rapidly, uncontrollably; I can't seem to breathe. What is he talking about? This can't be real. What does he mean by dressing up? Is he gay?

I have no knowledge about any of this. I consider myself to be pretty well-rounded and well-read, but I'm completely ignorant here. I pull myself together and ask the only question that comes into my mind.

"Will I get sick?"

Looking straight at me, he allows just the corners of his mouth to edge up and he says, "No, you will not get sick." Then in some kind of professorial tone he suggests I do some research—like this is some conference I'm attending.

"I was trying to put distance between us so you wouldn't find out," he says in barely a whisper. Then he looks in my eyes briefly, lowers his eyelids, his voice cracking, and says, "I was afraid once you knew about this you wouldn't love me anymore."

I'm wringing my hands, not trusting my voice, looking for some kind of rule or past experience to help me figure out what to do. I'm a rule follower, I always do the right thing, but what is the right thing in this moment? None of this makes any sense and it scares me. Is he perverted? A psycho? What about how fast my heart is beating and how much I love him?

I need to get away from here; time to think; time to breathe. He wants me to come back tomorrow and he'll fix me lunch--like normal people. I hesitantly agree. And with that I drive out into a dark and stormy night, tears running down my cheeks.

It's eleven o'clock at night. The rain is flooding my windshield and I can barely see the road. I can't stop the tears and the rain is relentless. The combination renders me helpless. I try to find a hotel, but no one wants to rent a room to a woman with a dog. I'm on Route 1 outside Philadelphia. I can be in New Jersey in ten minutes. All I have to do is get on the expressway and go east. Yes, that's what I'll do. I'll go and never look back.

I can't be a part of this depraved and most definitely immoral lifestyle. What had I expected? To ride off into the sunset in his camper? What I know is I've tried everything I could to get him to love me. Isn't that what I've always done, for years and years—all those years I was married? Turning myself into whatever someone else wanted, expected.

I need a place to think, even a rest stop will work. I will not leave Q in the car by herself just so I can get a room. She has been my loyal companion as I've traipsed around chasing my hugger/dancer. I'm so grateful she can't talk; what a tale she would tell of my shame and unworthiness. This beautiful creature that wants nothing more than to be with me.

Doesn't that just describe me? Waiting, watching, panting, begging for just a treat, a kiss, a dance. But then I've always seen Q as a regal beast, a queen. Whenever we are starting out on a trip and I'm packing up my bags, she paces for fear she is going to be left. I literally have to put her in the car hours before I'm ready to leave to reassure her she's going with me.

I wish Q could talk so she could tell me what to do. She's been through all of this turmoil with me, and she knows me so well. What does she make of this new pronouncement?

A guy who dresses in women's clothes. How does that work? Can't be all the time. I've been in his trailer; I've stayed over in his trailer, but I've never seen any women's stuff. There have been a few women's shampoos in the bathroom, but I figured they were castoffs from when his ex was there.

It makes absolutely no sense to me. My head is throbbing, both eyes and nose running. I see an exit up ahead. I'll pull off the road, park and try to pull myself together.

As the car slows down, I realize I haven't taken Q out of the car for hours. There is a gas station up ahead where I pull over. Getting her out isn't easy. My beautiful girl has bad hips, so I bought a ramp to help get her in and out of the car. I put on her leash and as we step out and head for a small patch of grass, her relief is immediate.

This wonderful companion of mine who never asks why or where or when we will be there. Her every need is met by my pat on her head, my inclusion of her on my trips, her need to be touching me as I'm watching tv or even when I'm stalking my lover. She never asks why; she makes no judgment of what I'm doing. She who knows all. She who can't speak. Imagine what she'd say if she could talk—this royal Labrador with the tell-all book. She'd probably make a fortune.

In the meantime, I have a big decision to make. I'm so confused I can't even decide for myself. I need to ask my dog to help me.

"What am I gonna do, Q? Just go back and have lunch, like we're normal people?" And then the oddest thing happens: Q throws up in the grass and starts to shudder. I'm afraid she's going to have some kind of seizure right here at the gas station.

Maybe I've asked too much of her, caused her too much stress, and then I realize we have been together so long, we're one. My agony, uncontrolled sobbing, and hysteria has affected her to the point it's made her physically ill. In that moment I realize what I must do. Gently I help her get back into the car and together we head out to a place that is both known and unknown. I wonder if I'm doing the right thing in this moment. I may be desperately searching for love and a safe place, but a sense of curiosity lies just below the surface of my madness.

CHAPTER 21
Sal

Journal Entry: June 15

I'm entranced, almost hypnotized by Sal. I can't seem to get enough of him—the loving, the touching, the hugging. That's pretty much all he needs to do for me. I sure must be love-starved. They used to tell me in the RV park that I had a better chance of getting struck by lightning than to ever find love at my age.

There's a deep sadness about him. I wonder if, had I more experience with love, I might have had a clue. We embrace, he tells me he loves me, and then his eyes say something else. He seems to be looking into my soul. If I ask him about this look, he says it's about his lifestyle and being a wanderer but it's more and it haunts me—like he's sorry for me, because I have the misfortune of loving him, someone who's not lovable, someone who's going to break my heart.

In retrospect, it was probably part of the allure, his need to be alone and that sad look in his eyes, and I guess it pulled me in. The look wasn't there all the time, just certain times when our love was intense. I knew he was torn—he wanted me, and he didn't want me. Little did I know how deep his own ambivalence ran.

At that time I had no idea he dressed in women's clothes. No idea how torn apart he was about loving me and also knowing he was bound to hurt me badly. Neither of us could have predicted then what would happen months later. In some ways it was a perfect storm: me with the impenetrable vines around my heart, and him, the north wind blowing everything away that tried to come near.

I was desperate to feel safe and be loved and he couldn't get away fast enough. One rainy, stormy night, no room in the hotel for the dog, my hugger/dancer just unburdens his soul to me. He's sure I'm gone for good—sure he's scared me away, that we're over. He goes back to what he always does: he covers the pain with alcohol. At that very minute, I make a U-turn, and go against every rule, boundary, and standard I have lived by my entire life.

CHAPTER 22
Beautiful and Flawed

Journal Entry: August 9

I've been spending so much time trying to get in my hugger/dancer's head—figure him out—analyze every word—and it's not helping me. My response is always to go to a bad place—the "he doesn't love me" place. Why do I do that? I've made this all about him, but what about me? What have I done to him? Have I committed to loving him unconditionally or have I decided to only go so far, which is why the coming and going worked for me?

Is that what I wanted—to just show up at his camper whenever I felt like it? Am I crying for me because I've refused to be with him totally and completely? What about my sense of superiority and the fact I have material possessions? Add that to my blowing in and out and bestowing gifts, what must that feel like for him?

But he is the one with the gift of love and he has bestowed it on me. I have nothing to give him compared to his gift, which I'm not ready to accept. Aha, it's out in the open. I'm crying for Kat because here is her chance and she's going to throw his love away and walk out because she's afraid of being vulnerable, afraid of getting hurt.

It's late but I take one last stab at getting us a place for the night. As I'm getting Q back in the car, I spot a Red Roof Inn across the street from the gas station. When I go into the office, the desk clerk says, "Yes, we have rooms and yes, your dog is welcome." I have to stop myself from kissing the clerk's hand. I go out to the car, get Q, and we settle in for the night. I'm pretty sure I'm not going to be able to sleep, but Q's snoring already so I snuggle into bed. I sleep fitfully, tossing and turning and then...

I'm at the campground, in front of Sal's camper. It's exactly as it was earlier tonight but there is something different now. As I get out of the car, there's something wrong. The RV has two doors, but I only remember it having one. It's definitely the right camper.

Squinting my eyes, I see there are signs over each door: One is clearly marked Perfect *while the other door says* Flawed. *I hesitate and begin to rummage through my purse, scattering my belongings around on the grass. Maybe I'll sit down on the picnic table and see if I can catch my breath. Then again, maybe I'll go back to the car, get Q out, and let her walk around.*

As I sit at the picnic table, my legs are all jumpy and my feet want to get up and run away. I look for my keys then I realize I no longer have keys to this camper. Is it possible there are no keys? Maybe once you make your decision to return and face this improbable situation, choosing which door to enter isn't so hard.

And just when I decide, the signs above the doors change. Now one says Beautiful *and the other* Mediocre. *This is bizarre. The strange part is I don't remember which door is which. Are the* Perfect *and* Beautiful *doors the same?*

Or is it the <u>Flawed</u> and <u>Beautiful</u>? Is it possible that once the signs on the door change, all bets are off?

If what was previously noted on the doors isn't a factor and I only have to choose between <u>Beautiful</u> and <u>Mediocre</u>, that's not even a contest. I've never considered myself beautiful but I'm pretty sure the <u>Flawed</u> door and the <u>Beautiful</u> door are the same door. That thought emboldens me. My breathing calms. I can do this. I can choose the <u>Flawed</u> door that just happens to also be the <u>Beautiful</u> door.

I've made up my mind—I'm going in the <u>Beautiful</u> door with my <u>Flawed</u> self. I am beautiful, flaws and all. I will bring along my paper bags for now. In the future I may buy my own set of Gucci bags, but I doubt it will happen. Paper bags are so much more practical plus they can easily be folded and stored and used again and again. Campers and paper bags— temporary yet permanent, year-round or seasonal, part-time or full-time—perfect for wandering or just staying put. Some paper bags are strong enough to hold a lifetime of memories.

As I turn the handle and open the door, I see what has been strategically placed in the middle of the couch, not to be missed—three beautiful, perfect, brand-new paper bags.

When I wake up in the morning, I remember the dream and I realize my perspective has changed since I'm no longer a predator or a stalker. I don't want to think about what a weird scene that was: me in my car in the teeming rain, lying in wait. I need to forgive myself; I was crazed and out of my mind. As I stuff that in my paper bags, I know I will revisit the scene again soon. This time I will use my lens of wonder—the one that says, "Bravo, you confrontational woman you!"

As I try to figure out my strange dream with all the doors, what starts to make the most sense are the paper bags laid out on the couch. I don't need a therapist to tell me what they mean. My psyche is telling me Sal's camper is where I belong. His presentation of the three perfect paper bags is the invitation. My dreams are telling me to open the door and enter with curiosity and wonder by my side.

"I thought you were gone for good. I never thought you would come back. I figured you wouldn't want any part of someone like me," Sal admits when we clutch each other tightly, me sobbing hysterically.

"I couldn't do it—I just couldn't walk away—I wanted to, so badly— but I just couldn't." We hold each other for hours. Later I say, "I don't know how to do this—how to live like this. You will have to show me, help me." And so, we would begin—just like normal people.

CHAPTER 23
Attraversiamo

There is really no other way I could have learned anything here. God gave me the love of my life and covered him in pain, challenging me to go beyond the surface and learn the lesson He has waiting for me. I still haven't learned the lesson, but I get it.

And the authenticity is the truth-telling part, telling myself the truth, beginning to understand my need to have a partner be flawed so that my focus can't be on myself, but on the flaws of another. Yes, it's easier to see someone else's flaws.

Mine are insidious because they look like goodness: perfection, people-pleasing, self-righteousness, judgment, etc. Most of them keep me outer-directed, searching always for another's response. Weighing my worth on another's response. I can only change by observing myself honestly. That is my intention for today.

Let's cross over…. Attraversiamo… As I'm crossing the threshold into the RV, this beautiful Italian phrase liberally sprinkled through Elizabeth Gilbert's *Eat, Pray, Love* grabs my attention and I roll it over and over across my tongue. I'm sure Elizabeth would approve of not only where the word resides in me but more importantly what the word has come to mean to me.

Let's cross over, together. My beau has already crossed, I'm the hesitant one. Unable to reconcile the morality, this is Catholic school, on top of an Irish calling from God, nuns, priests, kneeling to say my prayers, hats at church, white gloves, my mind is spinning. Not my heart; my heart is open and vulnerable. What I need is courage. The courage to *traversiamo.*

I see the paper bags, always present, a reminder of my gypsy lifestyle. My paper bags overflow with shame. The white gloves cannot mask the shame; it comes out of my pores and drips down my elbows. I now have a lover, a boyfriend. This nomenclature kind of thing is tricky. When you're married, it's your husband. We are living in sin—as more shame drips on the floor. I'd like you to meet my boyfriend—what are we, sixteen? Maybe we are. Yes, we're teenagers—in love as if we will never grow up. Clinging to some kind of dream with not a lick of any kind of sense. Now all my French lessons come together. I have a *beau*. In French *beau* means beautiful. A beautiful lover.

In my dreams I'm always young. Is it because I yearn to be young again? My friend Phyllis says it's because in our minds we are still young. My body is wrinkled but my spirit is flawless. Curious and wondering, my spirit is seeking truth. It urges me to be authentic. My spirit hands me a huge sponge she names "curiosity." Then she tells me to use it to mop up those drips as if my life depended on it. In my curious nature, I wonder just how big this sponge is? Will I be able to *traversiamo*? Maybe if I start with a little peek, a step, a glimpse. I know my spirit is willing. After all, we are just kids, adolescents, teens. We have dreams.

The beer dulls the ache; the dressing up in women's clothing gives him someone who can love him always and unconditionally; he's never alone or lonely. The distance he creates between us is meant to keep me at arm's length. The chairs positioned just so under the awning of the camper, the professorial tone of his voice, the suggestion I do some research. I'm going to need more information.

I'm so ignorant my first reaction is to laugh and say, "You're kidding, right?"

"No," he chides, "This is no joke and it's not even remotely funny."

Now something lodges in the back of my throat; a scream, panic, fear. Yes, it's fear; fear of the unknown, sickness, perversion. Little Kat is here and she gets right to self-protection. She needs to make sure I won't get sick. Her presence brings out the little boy who says, "I'm afraid if you know the truth, you will not love me."

So, here we are—me and my ambivalence and my hugger/dancer and his fatalism. He says, "I knew when you left that was the end of us, you'd never come back because I don't deserve love. I was sure I had lost you forever."

And then he opens my eyes to an alternative reality, different from anything I had ever known or experienced. His RV is filled with women's clothing, high heels, makeup, and lingerie. A teddy with a garter belt and stockings adorns the couch. Every surface is lovingly decked out with assorted lipsticks, nail polishes, even jewelry and fancy bags.

I've been here in this camper many times, but I never saw anything like this. Where has it all been hiding? Shocked by this admission, I wonder about the shame of it. "Do you feel shameful about all of this?" I ask.

"No, I enjoy it," he responds. "Every morning I have a tea party and I dress up with makeup."

While I am mesmerized by the array of femininity, I'm unsure whether I can make love to a man in a garter belt.

Most of all I need to think about how this affects me. My love is strong but there is to be no case study here. My curiosity, among other things, is aroused. He's a loner and a wanderer. He could take off at any time. How do I continue to love him, take the risk, and let go of whatever the bad stuff in my mind is telling me?

Accept—I have to accept that we'll have love as long as we have it, moment to moment. Then the writer makes a decision she can abide. Wonder and curiosity will be her companions. She'll write and she'll learn. All the while she'll be learning to love herself. She's going to need this self-love in the days to come as she witnesses her lover primping and strutting around, completely focused on the woman in the full-length mirror. This is why he can wander off like Lee Marvin in *Paint Your Wagon*—he takes his love with him.

This morning Sal got up and showered. When he came out, he had on lace panties. I figured he needed some space, so I went into the bathroom to give him room. Full regalia did not show up right away as he explained, "I was trying to judge your reaction to the panties first."

He puts on a bra, fastening the hooks in the front. Then sliding the clasps around to the back, he inserts silicone breasts into the cups. Next comes a camisole, stockings, a dress, and white pumps. This dressing up is done methodically and I'm fascinated. Not repulsed, I find I'm curious. I ask, "Are you aroused sexually by all of this?" "Do you usually masturbate?" And what is really on my mind, "Will this affect our sex life?"

His response stuns me: "I think my dressing up will enhance our sex. I'd like to take you to bed with me and my garter belt and stockings."

However, this will not be the day. Today he is leaving to visit his ex. I'll be left to ponder lovemaking to a man in lace panties. If I become part of this life, will he make love to me or to this other self, the one he sees in the mirror? Someone who's always there and never rejects him. Someone who even dresses the way he likes.

How much will I have to detach? Will my writing need to be fiction? After Sal leaves and I'm alone here in the camper, my writer's creativity takes over: How about a murder mystery where the protagonist is a detective? He's the only one who will be able to spot the clues: pride, vanity, doubt. The detective decides the motivation for the crime is anger and rage brought on by too much testosterone and not enough estrogen.

This is the mystery I concoct as I wait for my love to come back from his trip to visit his ex. An attempt at fiction to describe the predicament in which I'm living. This is where my mind goes:

The Evil Suspects

Just before I bought the gun, I made an appointment with the gynecologist. "So, how have you been sleeping," said Dr. Grab.

"Sleeping," I screamed. "Are you crazy? I haven't slept in months. The gun catalog beside my bed has been my only solace. Exactly what kind of hole did I want to make in his body, that's what kept me up at night."

The diagnosis was as I expected: rage brought on by a hormone imbalance. My friends suggest I take out a few people before I have the estrogen replacement prescription filled.

Here I am, a substantial, fiftyish woman with a hit list longer than a mafia family. I'm searching for wisdom and inner independence, yet my list of suspects includes evils like pride, vanity and doubt. At my age, these hardened criminals are more frightening than the gray pubic hairs I can never cover up.

And what are vanity and pride doing in this body anyway? Why do they hang on so, looking for validation? Doubt is something else; always there, always lingering, waiting for an opening.

What is the mystery? How clever—the mystery is my body. The wooing, the removal of clothing, the fiftyish body, vanity and pride—the evil suspects. All coming together to put me in my place. A clever writer, this is fiction after all.

163

When Sal returns I need to talk about how I'm feeling—my anxiety, apprehension, fascination, fear of the unknown, my doubts, and also my desires. I'm fragile, ambiguous, and unsure. He shares with me how he protects himself and keeps from getting hurt by keeping people at a distance.

I realize I've spent my whole life doing that and I'm not going to do it anymore. I'm going to live and love and take a risk on love. In some ways Sal would like to end our relationship; that would be the easier thing to do. He could look back on it as a loving memory and then go on with his rambling lifestyle.

Now that we've seen the obstacles, we wonder if maybe we have a chance. But then it's pretty clear how hard I can work on something. What would it look like if I didn't have to work on it? That would be the letting go, the not striving, the not trying to influence, not trying to make things happen. Accepting—why is that so hard for me? Yep, my self-esteem, which says, "You don't deserve to be happy, loved, cherished." And then I wonder how I'll be with lovemaking in drag—will I be able to be fully present without inhibitions?

I lovingly touch the lace and smooth it down over his thighs. Time is suspended. I can barely breathe; my heart is pounding in my ears. He whispers, "I've been waiting my whole life for this."

I help him fasten a locket at the back of his neck and a bracelet at his wrist. The bedroom is glowing, and I begin to understand why I love him. He has the heart of a woman, tender, sensitive, caring. He loves dancing, walking on the beach, cooking for me. I'm entranced by the rituals, the preparations for lovemaking, all the things I take for granted.

She makes herself beautiful for me and I open my heart to love. All my inhibitions fly out the window. I love her gently and carefully with my whole heart and soul. She is a man, she is a woman, she is love, and she comes to me and I say yes, yes, oh yes...

CHAPTER 24
Ambivalence

Journal Entry: September 10

    I need to think about how this affects me. My love for him is very strong, but he doesn't want to be anyone's case study. We talked a lot about us—more than we ever did. He talked about his not being stable, which I told him I knew from the beginning. That was part of the appeal—the devil-may-care attitude, the hedonistic live-for-today mantra. This was all new to me and I thrived on it.

    In fact, I was desperately trying to live in the moment, stay focused on the now. So, I told him I didn't need stability. He cautioned me he's a loner and could leave at any time. I don't think I can love him and protect myself from the pain of getting hurt and being left. I'm going to have to accept we'll have love today, right now, in this moment. Nothing else is promised.

    Ambidextrous: the ability to swing a bat, golf, or play tennis with either hand. Can those people also write with either hand? "Ambi," the prefix, as in either or. Ambisexual? Is that even a word, an option? What about bisexual? Bisexual means you can go either way. So, would ambisexual mean a proclivity such as right-handed or left-handed? Is one way preferable, even God-given? Just as parents used to pattern their children to be righties, would future parents urge their children to be ambisexual? If there is an advantage in sports to be a lefty, could ambisexuality be a different kind of advantage? Yes, I'm very curious.

Ambivalence is the word that gets me here. That and the fact that gender pronouns no longer fit, are considered limiting. Always a tomboy, I was raised with three brothers and I never threw a ball like a girl. Should that have been some kind of warning? When girls screamed while being chased by boys, I held my ground and thought the other girls were dumb to run. I put my hands on my hips and scoffed in the boys' faces.

Truth be told, I had my hair cut by a barber when I was twelve. I remember sitting in the old hotel lobby while the men were getting clipped, my stomach clinched in terror when the barber would flip on the switch of the clippers. The hair on the back of my neck never had a chance to be anything but stubble. It never occurred to me to protest or refuse. One did not disobey my mother. Later I would lie, cheat, drink, smoke, fornicate, but not on this day.

The barber must have felt sorry for me, but he had his orders, the ones I repeated verbatim. "Tell him it's to be short all over. None of that hanging down stuff in the back. I want it clippered on the sides and in the back. He can let you have some bangs." The "hanging down stuff" was what all the other girls had—pageboys, flips, ponytails. I did get the bangs, but they were not to be in my eyes. "Above the eyebrows," demanded my mother.

I never really understood why I couldn't have longer hair, even chin length, but it was forbidden, not even up for discussion. I did have beautiful bologna curls that bobbed up and down when I was three years old. Apparently after four children, my mother decided everyone, including me, should have short, clippered hair. I would let my hair grow in college and find out I had beautiful, thick, wavy, and flowing locks. For most of my life, however, I would continue to keep my hair short. A nod to practicality, I guess. Never one to spend hours in the salon, it seems like a waste of time.

In my twenties my hair starts to turn white. I have a patch of white against a sea of dark brown that continues to spread across the top and left side of my head. By the age of forty-five, all of the front of my hair is white and in the back salt and pepper. I never consider having it dyed: too much fussing, too high maintenance. The fact is I never primp or fuss; a little moisturizer, blusher, and I'm good. I take pride in the fact I can be ready in ten minutes.

Boyfriends comment, "You're such a good sport," when they call at the last minute and ask me out. I take it as a compliment. Every significant male relationship in my life, with the exception of one, started out as a last-minute date. Yes, his name was Jerry, the most beautiful man I had ever seen. He asked me out a week in advance and you know how I rewarded him for his thoughtfulness.

Because "ambi" words seem to haunt me, a word like "ambivalent" gets stuck in my head and I start to wonder if I'm ambivalent in the context of sexuality. Is it possible I'm attracted to women? Unless it's buried really deep, it seems doubtful. I cannot deny, however, I am sexually stimulated by seeing her dressed in lace panties. Is it only because I love her so much or are the feminine clothes the turn-on? Yes, I'm curious—*bi-curious* even. Now there's a name for my kind of curiosity. It's a double whammy. As a writer, I'm innately curious; as a woman I have a newfound wonder about soft and silky fabrics.

I never did understand when men and women would talk about "getting lucky." It never seemed like hitting the jackpot at the casino, or making the coverall in bingo. It wasn't until the rapture that I understood. Here in this moment, the hotel barber with the clippers, the closely shaven back of my white hair, the lack of lipstick and makeup, none of it seems to matter. There are two people and there is love. What else really matters?

I'm a woman who makes love to a man dressed like a woman. I don't even need foreplay; lace panties and a push-up bra laid out on the bed signal my body to start producing fluid. My pulse quickens and I start to quiver. There must be something seriously wrong with me; maybe I'm perverted. Maybe I'm a lesbian. But I know I like boys; I've always liked wild boys.

I need some rules, here in this trailer, in this bed. Where can I go to find the boundaries? What can I read to help me understand what my body wants so desperately? Who can I ask to help me with my struggle to do what's right? The right thing—I've always done the right thing—I said my prayers, I stayed married, I was the perfect wife. But, always, there was something missing. Passion and self-love were just out of reach. In my prayers, I asked God to show me how to find love in my heart, the heart covered in vines. God has a sense of humor—he gives me love dressed up in pink lace panties.

"Here's your love," He says. "Now you figure it out." It all defies reason. Practical and methodical, I'm a Virgo. I like organization, systems, and patterns. Never good at math in school, I'm amazed to find out I can do numbers in my head. *1* is a woman, *1* is a man, add them up and you have a couple. What if the *1* really wants to be a woman? How does that compute? Still a couple? How does the desire of *1* figure into the equation?

This is not the kind of math you have in school, at least not in public school. Catholic school makes it much clearer: One man plus one woman equals a family. Ok. I like that—succinct, unambiguous—rules. There is, however, one problem—my body. I can't stop the desire or the liquids.

Ambivalent, I'm at war with myself. I'm in love but I'm sure it's wrong—wrong gender, wrong setting. I'm supposed to be married, not living in sin, in a trailer in the woods. When you have a secret, a camper works out very well. Isolation is key. I never have to worry about someone knocking on my door in the neighborhood. There are no neighbors, no friends to hurry up and wipe the lipstick off before he answers the door. An isolator at heart, I chalk it up to my writer's need for peace and quiet. In my paper bags, with the curiosity, I get a glimpse of a woman who has everything to hide.

As the secrets tumble out, I begin to see my heart and the crumbling wall. On the surface I'm put together—nice smile, friendly, and welcoming. Don't get too close. I won't let you in. Distant, aloof, and perfect, I'm unreachable. Panic sets in when I have no rules for how I'm about to live. I'm torn apart by the love I feel with my whole body versus the thinking part of me that has always been in charge. Intellectually, I know this setting is wrong, but the pull of my body is stronger than my will to do the right thing. I fall deeply in love.

Dirty talking is something new for me, but I get the hang of it pretty quickly. It does, along with all our lovemaking, require a certain vulnerability. If you prefer to be straddled, ravaged, and dominated, you need to know that I have become the Alpha. I'm the dominator, I do the straddling. I much prefer this role to the lady in white gloves in the missionary position.

Would she prefer to be with a man? We have not talked about this, mostly because I don't really want to know. Yes, I may be the Alpha, but I continue to be non-confrontational. She is a woman in a man's body. Because of this, there is a certain discontent, a need to wander, to hitch up her wagon, to go anywhere except where she is right now.

We are both learning to live with this undercurrent of yearning. Transgender surgery does not seem to be an option. Whether it is age-related, I don't know. What I do know is she has not told anyone. It's a secret. I've only ever told my sister Liz. How lucky for me to have a therapist for a sister. Her answer is always, "Kat, God doesn't care what kind of panties he wears."

CHAPTER 25
Pronouns

Journal Entry: October 1

    It takes a lot of work if you want to be a friend of mine. Dora Jane seems to be up to the challenge. She talks nonstop so it never occurs to her I'm not open and vulnerable. Every thought she has comes out of her mouth in a rambling stream of consciousness. She inserts herself into my life with such good-natured vulnerability, I can't push her away. Maybe if I slip by her RV in my kayak, I can ditch her, but instead, she buys a kayak and paddles after me.

    Dora Jane, a Southern debutante, charms herself into my life. She would never understand this "he"/"she"/"they"/"them" pronoun controversy. She, of the "never met a stranger" philosophy—the "calls me every day" kind of friend. Me, who hates talking on the phone. Me, who doesn't need anyone. Me, who when she lies dying, never tells her my secret.

❖

Notice the pronoun Liz used when she said, "It doesn't matter what kind of panties he wears"—before *he* and *she* became so limiting. Today Liz would say, "God doesn't care what kind of panties 'they' wear." It's her job to stay neutral, especially with gender. Confusing times? To be right in the middle of the polarity and to keep it a secret seems to be too much to ask.

Now I know how important the paradox is in the whole process of creating. In systems thinking, you try to hold the "not knowing" because as Peter Senge says, "That is where the real creativity lies." The creative process of writing employs the polarities: On one hand you have what is—the reality—on the other you have what you want, what you pine for, the end of the rainbow.

What if you have the pot of gold but you don't know it? Can a story flesh it out? I'm hoping it's possible. I've been to Lilydale and had a glimpse of my future—the palm trees. The only other specifics I remember was a mention of the creator of Garfield the Cat. I get nothing to link that up to except the ears and cat ears just don't compare to rabbit ears, although….

When you're raised to be nice, smile, and be perfect, loving someone with a penis and calling him "she" or "her" is forbidden territory. In the 60s, I'm in high school and there are rules. I'm a whiz in English class. My specialty is pronouns. I know exactly when to use *he* and *she*. "A woman draws a line between her and her husband." Most people write, "between she and her husband," which sounds right but is not grammatically correct. When I parse out the words in my sentence diagram, I go back to the word "between" to get the gist of this grammar stuff. I'd get that part right. What confuses me is when do I use the pronoun *she*—only when she wears the fishnet stockings?

Diagramming sentences and avoiding dangling participles are no challenge for me. I love rules, patterns, and just about any logical order or sequence our English teacher requires us to learn. Memorize the nineteen lines of "Evangeline" by Henry Wadsworth Longfellow? Done. "This is

the forest primeval, the murmuring pines and the hemlocks, bearded…."
Once learned, never forgotten.

Turns out, I'm not alone in the confusion. My sister Liz says, "In my practice here in California, after a session, I ask my client if her friend is giving her a ride home. I say, 'Are *they* picking you up?' Male and female pronouns are not used here; they're seen as limiting." Maybe we should live in LA.

Because I'm desperate for rules, I'm learning a new language. My first book *Needless to Say* was at one time titled *The Language of Needs*. Titles can be tricky just like pronouns. I need a whole new vocabulary with strict guidelines on the exact word to use when I'm complimenting ah, *them* on the sexy outfit.

My solution, a romance language—French. *Parlez vous…* This is a logical conclusion since we live amidst many French Canadians who are snowbirds. I'm in awe of their love of life. They're happy people who love to dance, sing, and enjoy life. They bring a sense of vitality and I long to join in their frivolity.

Being a modern woman, I download an app to learn French. Daily I practice on the computer. When I go to the pool the French gather and chat together in a circle. I don't understand a word they say. Smiling my all-purpose smile, I vow a language barrier will not stop me. More than anything, I'm curious about why they're laughing, why they're having so much fun, and why they look so *tres contente*.

Now the Americans have fun, but this is something different, something special. Boisterous, joyful, and full of glee, the French Canadians seem to live life to the fullest. And as much camaraderie as I witness, I also notice people who are best buddies this year don't speak to each other next year. Hmmm…. Must have something to do with the passionate way they live. While I'm leery, I want what they have. And so, I study their language.

Apps can teach you almost any language, but I struggle with the approach. They don't start with the rules. How am I supposed to learn if they don't tell me "with a feminine word you put an e on the end of the word?" I have to find this out for myself. Oh, right, it's free. You figure out the rules as you go along. This is starting to sound familiar.

As I work through the lessons, getting more curious as the days go on, a pattern starts to appear. Clearly *elle* (she) is feminine and *il* (he) is masculine. But what about *ils* and *elles*— the plurals? Why not just one word for "they"? From what I can gather without rules to guide me, each can be the word "they." What? I thought I would find a way through my confusion by using a different language and I'm right back where I started.

Chair (*chaise*) is feminine, wine (*vin*) is masculine. Inanimate objects have gender. To make it more confusing, verbs and adjectives must have gender agreement. Ah, "gender agreement"; I certainly need a rule here. If the French could agree on wine and a chair, then the two of us could settle this "he/she" thing by agreeing on the appropriate circumstance to use the word. There are soft, elegant, pretty times and there are powerful, towering, handsome times.

As I delve deeper into romance, I learn there are rules for "grammatical gender" and how to "pair" nouns and other parts of speech. I'm all about "pairing," so if I can assign gender to specific scenes—lovemaking, "she"; watching football, "he"; cooking together….? Now I'm stuck again. Maybe this isn't hard for other people. I have so many paper bags to unload; only so much curiosity to free myself from all the vines around my heart. There is love and courage behind the wall. How deep will I have to go to find it?

I decide to ask my French acquaintances if they can help me with the gender confusion I'm experiencing, i.e., maybe some rules about how to determine if a word is masculine or feminine. One says, "You're just going to have to memorize what is feminine because there are no obvious standards." Great.

So, I'm waiting to go out to play tennis and I ask another Canadian friend, "Any ideas you can give me to help me with the gender endings in French?"

He says, "You need to check out the *Academie Francaise*—the people who determine everything about the French language—they are the guardians of the words. I hear they're having some controversy among themselves as to what is to remain French and what is in danger of being changed because of the current gender-neutral atmosphere. From what I've heard, there may be changes afoot. Check the internet and see what you can find under *Academie Francaise.*"

As I delve into this issue, it turns out the highest French language authority believes there is a conspiracy afloat to bastardize the language by simplifying the gender confusion. The *Academie Francaise* is comprised of forty individuals called *les immortels.* No, you don't need to learn French to understand the words—the immortals. Sounds similar to the Supreme Court, right? To date, there have been 732 *immortels*, nine of whom have been women. The first woman was elected to the *Academie* in 1980.

None of this is helping me one iota. I'm still getting kicked off my app when I make too many errors because of gender confusion. It should be noted, however, that other writers must have made similar mistakes since Sartre, Rousseau, Balzac, Descartes, and Proust were not members of this vaunted authority. If Proust was alive today, I wonder what he would make of this *quel scandale.*

"Without genders, there will be chaos," warns the *Academie.* Without genders how would we know who to nominate for the revered *Academie*?

To which I add curiously, what will happen when my friends find out I'm in love with a woman? That I have a *beau*? A beautiful lover?

I was so hoping French would be the answer. Now all I have is more questions and I wonder what other writers think about this conundrum, this "inclusive writing," the confusion and illegibility—a rift in the *Academie.* Why are some authors chosen but others rejected? A love of language and a curious search for a language, a way to express the love I feel, brings me to French, a romantic language.

As I write and learn French, I'm reminded of the *tres bien* company I'm in—those French literary giants who were never members of the *Academie*, never became *les immortels:* Jules Verne, Emile Zola, Gustave Flaubert and Moliere. Never candidates, maybe rejected or possibly even died before there was a vacancy—would their addition have made a difference?

When we're different, not the norm, language can hurt us. Some writers seek to lessen the harm by neutralizing the disparity with language. Others seek another language altogether. I happen to be one of the seekers, the curious, of the "I wonder" ilk. I have a *beau. Tu es beau*—You are beautiful. *Je t'adore*—I love you.

CHAPTER 26
The Writer

Journal Entry: October 5

So, what do I want to write? Do I want to write about my life? Liz seems to think it would be worthwhile. She likes the Baja experience, seeing me jumping off the boat into the choppy seas as a metaphor for my life. But how could I do anything with that except write about it? Would I get pleasure and satisfaction? Would I do it to help others or would I do it for myself? Would I be doing it for something to do—would it be for self-development and growth? Would that be enough?

Can I just "be" instead of having to be something, do something? Have I felt less than because I wait for my hugger/dancer to get up and I wait for him to come home from work? Am I not getting on with my life? What is my life? What is my path? If it's the path of love, then doesn't he have to be here, with me? Problem! I need to be here for me—to love me.

Yes, the drinking is a problem, but I have no control over it. I have three options: accept, change, leave. The only one I can change is me. Now "accept" doesn't mean holding in the back of my mind that someday he'll stop drinking. And it doesn't mean accepting things that are not acceptable. The literature says the disease will progress; he'll start drinking more until he gets sick. My first grandchild is coming in a few months. I can no longer pretend. I may need him in an emergency, and I can't count on him the way things stand. In the morning I'll tell him I can't live like this anymore.

<u>*Journal Entry: October 20*</u>

I do my nails—that's about as close as I get to keeping the focus on me. So, why is that? Do I truly not need to have him look at me because my self-esteem is low, and I'll accept anything I can get from him? I imagine he sees it much differently than I do. It's not meant to take away from me or his love for me, it's just the attraction he feels for himself as a woman is very strong and there's a newness to it.

He loves to see me checking him out like a guy would do to a girl. And I find myself doing exactly that. Because he has beautiful legs and he feels so sexy, it turns me on. I don't think I'm manipulative, but I do know it's possible, because the hole inside of me is so looking to be filled.

"Check the label and see how much Lycra and spandex those stockings have, would ya? I like them to really hold me in when I put them on—the tighter the better." Then Sal leans over the lingerie counter and whispers, "I love that feeling of everything being held tightly together."

The scene is right before my eyes: She's standing in front of the full-length mirror, in an obscenely short poofy skirt and spiky high heels, an outfit no one wears anymore unless they're working a street corner.

"Well, I'd die for legs like yours," I say, "and with those short skirts—incredible."

As I'm poring over the fabric content of the myriad of nylon stockings on the rack, I remember other shopping trips: my mother looking at thread count to decide which set of sheets to buy. My mother spending hours choosing fabrics she would drape across her dress form at home. My mother fondling the chintzes, velvets, and cottons, while I'm swirling around in a skirt made of dazzling gold lame. Outrageous amounts of money were spent on plaids and prints that were always colorful and arty. It was nothing for her to spend $5 on a button in the 1950s. This extravagance in a family that had no money.

Then she would turn the fabrics into outfits the likes of nothing our town had ever seen. Most of the time she didn't even use patterns. She'd pick up the fabric, hold it at arm's length, scrunch up her eyes like she was trying to get a picture of what the dress would become, and before you knew it, she'd get an idea. Now there was only she and her dress form, and the two of them made a happy couple. She'd have the straight pins in her lips, humming along to some '40s tune, and she'd be whisked away to another time and place. In some ways we had two mothers: the creative dress designer/singer and the rear end admiral who required complete surrender of our wills.

Wait, that's not the book I want to write. A book of fiction with the handsome detective will make a much better story. Our hero will need a macho job, maybe a Clark Kent/Superman storyline—mild-mannered cop turns into stiletto-heeled siren. Flashbacks would include his first dress as he pulls it from his mother's closet and twirls around and around. A complex man who is a gourmet cook, baseball fanatic, NASCAR junkie. His sensitive and caring nature glimpsed as in the bumbling of the famous investigator Columbo, stumbling across clues completely missed by his coworkers. Crime-fighting is feminized, and sex crimes are solved by the telltale hint of just a faint spot of ruby red nail polish left behind on the edge of the bathroom counter.

Then there's the NASCAR driver, steeped in the pomp and circumstance revolving around the racetrack—bright colors, costumes, pageantry. The polarity of the redneck sport with lace foundations, while implausible, would certainly be fun. Speed, crashes, violence, risk on the testosterone side; nurturing teams, the concept of "we," adoring fans, and loyalty on the feminine side—secrets kept from owners, lace panties under the tight-fitting uniforms emblazoned with Auto Plus, Day's Candy, Loyal Insurance. Never once an advertisement for lingerie or anything soft; the closest we get is fabric softener. With the current decline in NASCAR attendance, maybe a nod to feminization is just what is needed to update this sport.

Is it possible dressing up in women's clothing could encourage a softer, more feminine side, leading to nurturing, sensitivity, and just more loving kindness? How could that be bad? If it leads to sexual stimulation and more erotic sex, would that be bad? Could it lead to physical harm? Would it go against God's word? Does God really care what kind of panties I wear?

What about the sexual energy generated by seeing my man in lace panties? What's important and intentional from my writer's standpoint is the vulnerability, sensitivity, and nurturing that soft and silky fabrics encourage. Vulnerability takes courage. I'm opening myself to a new experience, something forbidden, scorned, misunderstood. Yet, it's only clothing. Why is it so scary? It's frightening because I can't connect it to anything I've ever experienced. It's taboo for men and women to want to experiment with each other's clothing.

The softness of the fabrics as they caress the skin, silks that slide over their hips, satins that glide across the thighs. As women we take this all for granted. It isn't until he says, "Oh my, that velvet wants to become my second skin as it hugs my body," that I stop for just a second and record in my writer's brain—a voice, a longing, for something beautiful, luxurious.

I recognize the voice; it pines to be surrounded with fluffy clouds, to be enveloped in a satin quilt of safety, to be encompassed in love and the fabric of choice. It's not the fabric that matters. It's the giving of oneself to another that is the ultimate gift.

Many soft and silky gifts will be given lovingly. I will fall in love with the NASCAR driver, the detective, and possibly even the aliens who are taking over the feminization of the planet in the sci-fi thriller coming out in the fall. "Write what you know," they say. "Write about your passion."

I jump off a boat into the choppy, swirling Sea of Cortez, become part of a living holograph as thousands of manta rays artfully glide through the water, and I swim with the big male sea lions. All of this portends the courage I'll need in the times to come. With this newfound courage I choose to be vulnerable, to be open to love and loving, and to write—about what I know.

CHAPTER 27
Regret

Journal Entry: November 13

    I guess what I've always done is focus on another. Sure, in my mind I'm reflective, but in my actions, I'm responding and reacting and always watching another's response for clues to how I ought to act. Interesting that before we left the Keys, I told my yoga teacher, Bonnie, "This is as far as I'm going."

    Amazing for me—saying what is best for me. Now this statement refers to my physical body and what yoga poses I'll try and what ones I figure are too hard—positions my body wasn't made for. Not only can I recognize what doesn't work for my body, but I can clearly say, "Hey, this doesn't work for me."

    I'm beginning to see how yoga heals. When I'm quiet, holding a pose, listening to my breathing for clues about what my body wants, I start to understand what I need. While I can't get to my needs through my brain, I can get there by listening to my body.

    The clues I watch for are my breath, when it speeds up or when I'm actually *holding it. My heart rate is harder to detect but I can always check my pulse. The key to everything is to get quiet. I can't hear my body if I'm talking.*

I'm lounging by the pool, paging through a magazine, trying to fill all the hours in the day, and yearning for some kind of production. My life has become hedonic and shallow. I have no purpose other than pleasure and fun. I can hear my mom's voice saying, "Don't just stand there, start folding clothes."

The unending baskets of clean clothes that sat in the upstairs hall begging to find their way into our drawers, just somehow never moved beyond the hallway. Those containers became our bureau drawers; when you wanted something, you rooted through the baskets. I was methodical in my search while the boys just tossed aside clothes onto the floor. That meant refolding those discarded clothes. It was a never-ending task. But, right then, by the pool, I desperately needed something productive to do.

Can I call myself a writer if I don't write? Can I be an author if I'm not published? Can I call myself productive if I'm lounging by the pool? The teacher says to be a writer, I have to "show up."

Now, I have brain game apps on my phone the same way kids have video games. My terror is I'll lose my mind like my dad. A gifted mathematician, he had to be locked in his bedroom at night to keep him safe. It was heartbreaking to see. Because I'm worried too, I take the spit test to find out if I have the Alzheimer's gene. Turns out I don't, but not having the gene doesn't mean I won't get the dreaded disease. The odds are better though.

How do I do with odds? There are those who say, "I can beat those odds," and there are the folks who believe there's "gotta be something wrong with those odds." Actually, I'm more of the research and study and lower the odds of getting the dreaded disease. I pore over the work of Dr. Dale Bredesen, *The End of Alzheimer's,* and I start fixing what Bredesen calls the "thirty-six holes in the roof"—a clever way to refer to a very complex disease. Right now, I have about twenty holes covered through supplements, avoiding sugar, eating fermented foods like kefir, lowering blood pressure, and decreasing inflammation by staying away from processed foods. As a Virgo, I'm regimented, so I gravitate to routine and organization. Thirty-six holes—I'm working on it.

I'm also working on regret. Regret is a powerful thing. Change is hard, but regret overpowers change. I want to change the way I have to overthink everything. I'm so deeply entrenched in right and wrong, he and she, girl pants and boy pants, where can I go with regret? "You'll be sorry when I die," my mother used to whine. "Don't cry for me then, it'll be too late."

I don't want to regret I didn't love completely. If I can change my odds of getting Alzheimer's, I can change how I look at loving Sal.

In an attempt to keep my brain active, I've been teaching folk dancing. The combination of movement and knowing the right step in the dance activates the cerebral cortex, keeping those neurons firing. It's also good for my work on being imperfect. I'm not sure if it's because of the Alzheimer's protocol I follow, but I have the ability to remember dance steps.

I'll be teaching a dance class and forget the next steps; I smile at my students and we all laugh. What I'm finally learning is no one wants to be friends with someone who's perfect or to love someone who's perfect. When I'm open and vulnerable and not afraid to show the real me, I'm more likable and people want to be around me.

I always thought I didn't want or need friends; I'm the solitary type, the writer who wants to be alone. Since I've opened my heart, my life has become fuller. My smile is still big but there's not enough polish in the world to make my teeth sparkling white again. Sure, I could get them chemically whitened but I kind of like this new imperfect look of mine. If I can accept my less-than-perfect teeth, my missteps on the dance floor, and my imperfections as a mother, I might just be able to surround myself with people like me. I could be leading or following, but one thing is for sure, my imperfect self and I will be dancing.

Lee Ann Womack sang it, Mark D. Sanders and Tia Sillers wrote it, "I Hope You Dance." That sense of wonder and the need to continue to learn—what a gift that is. Mom instilled in all of us a love of learning. She also loved to dance and sing. I still remember all the songs of the '40s she would sing as she danced around the house holding the fabrics she purchased for the dress form. "Sweet Georgia Brown" was one of her favorites.

I hope she's dancing and singing today in heaven. Yes, heaven. My mom did what she thought was right even though she was damaged too. She was right about so many things, but her methods were skewed by her own fears. She was, however, always strong on curiosity and wonder, and I believe the pair, along with good intentions, paves the way and opens the gate.

Sharing the load is another foreign concept. You're telling me you will go to the grocery store and get my food, and I balk. Trust someone else to get me what I need? Do I have to ask for it? Let me see if I get this right—I sit down at the table and you serve me the food you've shopped for and now cooked for me. And I struggle with all of it. Not worthy of being treated this well, I look for ways this won't work. It's not the brand I like, it's not the recipe I like for coleslaw, I don't do it like this, and on and on. How can I let someone lovingly take care of me? It seems wrong.

I've always been the one to care for everyone else, so this feels strange. And then finally I let it all go. Why would I fight it when someone wants to love me in this way? But that need to always be right, to do everything yourself, to not let anyone help, is the hallmark of perfectionism. I dance and I teach the steps and miss the downbeat and laugh. Then I look over my shoulder at the class, start to giggle, put my hand over my mouth, and we start all over again.

And that's what curiosity and inquiry do when you bring them into your life—forget the judgment and regret, they aren't helpful—open those paper bags and let in the wonder.

CHAPTER 28
The Christmas List

Journal Entry: December 15

Now I have The Boy, but in many ways, I've become The Boy. How ironic. I search my entire life and fate turns me into The Perfect Boy. I become the Alpha, the protector, the patriarch.

I have stability, independence, and The Boy. The only problem is, I have no experience with any of this. My life has always existed on what others want— certainly not what I want or need. I have much to learn.

Do I fear change? Abandonment? Commitment? Surrender? They all seem to be somehow connected to the addictions. Do the addictions hold us together? In my marriage, there was a scale between us, but it held us together. Is this the same pattern? A pattern with seeds planted in paper bags? Can the writer's curiosity find a way to open the bags, let out the seeds, and be authentic? With wonder and a rebellious nature, it is starting to look like it might be possible.

❖

It's been almost three years since the doctors removed Q's spleen, part of the cutting they did to get out the big tumor in her stomach. At the time we were in a campground north of Philly and she could not stop throwing up. I thought maybe she was eating grass that had some kind of chemicals on it, but the sickness went on way too long.

One day she got so weak, she couldn't get up, so we took her to see a vet my daughter used for their dog Casey. A few X-rays later and the doctor told me they needed to operate immediately. I agreed to the surgery even though I gasped audibly when the vet told me how much it would cost. There was never any question we would go ahead with the procedure.

When we picked her up, Q was in pretty bad shape. The vet suggested she be taken to an emergency hospital where they had twenty-four-hour care. At the desk they asked me to leave my credit card. I balked at first. I had never heard of anything like that. *Can they do this*, I wondered? But I went ahead and told them to please keep Q comfortable.

The nurses must have taken great care of her because the next day she was able to leave and go back with us to our camper. The RV steps were impossible to manage so Sal and I placed beach towels under her and lifted her into the trailer. This ritual would go on for a while before Q could manage the steps.

Later I bought a ramp so she wouldn't need to climb the steps. She recovered completely from the surgery, which they told us was very successful. They had neglected to mention, however, that the chance the tumor was malignant was fifty-fifty. I had never been given that info. I like to think I would have made the exact same decision had I known. As it turned out, her tumor was benign.

Now, she's not doing well; her legs hardly work at all. The vet said it's arthritis. I've tried everything—pills, shots, massages, food—but nothing seems to work. Getting in and out of the camper is the hardest part. This morning I'm getting ready for tennis so getting Q out of the camper is going to be a problem. She stopped eating a couple days ago, can't control her bladder, and has been wetting the floor. It's heartbreaking to see. When I come down to the kitchen, her head is down and she's just lying there. I get down close to her on the floor, and her tail starts to wag.

I give her loving pats and try to reassure her things will be ok.

"Christmas is coming," I say. "What are you hoping for?"

Last night Sal and I made out our wish lists, which we posted on the fridge. I'm not good at wanting gifts so I usually write down practical things like tennis balls. I try to tell Q about our lists, but she's trying to get up on her feet. This is so hard to watch so I get behind her and give her a boost. When she gets on her feet, I try to steer her to the door so I can get her outside, but she seems to have a different idea. She's pulling me toward the refrigerator. What is she doing?

Q nuzzles my arm and pulls at my hand, guiding me. I'm confused until she takes her nose and puts it right in the middle of my Christmas list. Right where the words "tennis balls" and "kayak gloves" are crossed out. In their place is one word with a checkmark next to it: husband.

I have to look at the list twice before I get it. Sal has scratched out my practical gift ideas and written in a word that surely takes me by surprise. This is how he's telling me.

Q and I go down the ramp but only one of us will come back in. I sit with her for what seems only minutes as life leaves her. My beautiful companion who only ever wanted to be with me. To be safe, to feel safe— all either of us ever wanted.

CHAPTER 29
Immutable

Journal Entry: December 30

At first I say yes to marriage, then my practical self takes over. It's not smart, not a good financial move. I'm so afraid to unwrap my hands from my purse, the one I clutch so tightly. Afraid if I'm not careful, all my savings will be gone and all we'll have is social security. Afraid if I don't have a stash, I won't be able to continue to be the Alpha.

I like this role even though it means I have to take care of everything. I have no more excuses; now I have to take care of myself. No more giving my power to anyone else. Even though I'm still fearful, I accept I am in charge of my own life. I acknowledge I am a complete person. I am courageous.

The decision against marriage, however, is not courageous. I believe I'll regret it. Practicality reigns. Would marriage resolve the yearning? There's a deep discontent that can't be healed by me or any rite or ritual. I'm trying to keep my focus on me, not on someone else. I do know we're better off together. We love each other and while we're not united legally, we are committed to this fragile union.

❖

Immutable—not able to change. Words are powerful. "Fixed," but what about "willing to change"? Am I unwilling to change? Am I immutable? Are we both immutable? If it's true, we're lost. I don't believe love conquers all. I'm a romantic but even I don't believe in fairy tales.

I'm way too concerned with pleasing others, too worried what others will think, too steeped in what others believe about right and wrong. I've always been a thinker, but I've stayed in my head, not on the battleground. I can count on one hand the number of times I stood up for myself and what I believe. I have no experience in this realm.

Now I'm wondering if my story is my chance, an opportunity for understanding that because someone dresses differently it doesn't mean they're perverted or dangerous. They may be a man with the soul of a woman. Why would that ever be something threatening? It's scary because it goes against what I've been taught to believe is right—it doesn't follow the rules, the ones I grasp so tightly.

All around me everything I believe in is disintegrating—institutions, government, health care. When someone flaunts their clothing in my face, a man dressed as a woman or a woman dressed as a man, I balk because this is not the way it's supposed to be. This is someone who's not hiding, someone who's in my face.

Why does she have to hide? I understand the need to be flamboyant because these are times when the only way to get attention is to stand up and stand out. My hugger/dancer never got to be a teenaged girl, never got to wear outrageous clothes, short skirts, suggestive tops—she's making up for it now.

And then Sal says, "Imagine how it feels to not be in your own body, to want to be someone else—my whole life I've wanted to be a woman."

In my ignorance I thought the fact that I tolerated, even encouraged the dressing, bought her nighties and soft silky things, was enough.

Here I am, living two lives and keeping secrets, yet there's an undercurrent of unease and yearning. I feel content in our love and our relationship, but my hugger/dancer is always searching for something new, a trip, a concert, a getaway. I know the discontent is within him; it never occurs to me the depth of the source of the wanting. I worry it's about me—I'm not enough, he needs to get away from me.

But what would going away accomplish? When we do have time away from each other and he goes away for a week, the time spent apart and the missing each other is intense. As he's leaving, he says, "It's getting harder and harder to separate from you, but I'm sure once I get twenty miles down the road, I'll be fine."

And there you have it—the *Paint Your Wagon Sequel*. The difficulty is the parting. Once gone, he can go right back to being the loner and wanderer. This time with no one to bother him with silly questions about contentment. This parting scenario is always hanging over our heads. Each of us has our own idea how it will happen. Since we're both damaged, it's only a matter of time before we make it come true.

So, I have love but I'm sure it won't last. She loves me but down deep she knows any day or anytime I'm going to tire of the dressing and the secrets. We're a paper-bag pair: kept for practicality, but bound to be discarded eventually.

Yes, I know—she needs me and that's not a good reason to stay together. But I need her too. I feel safe with her. I can say whatever comes into my mind and I don't have to worry about being corrected or criticized. It's so wonderful not to have to rehearse every conversation a million times to get up the nerve to ask or make a comment, to not have to weigh everything I say for fear of being derided or verbally abused.

When something pops up in my mind, I just spit it out. I'm not afraid of how she will respond. It's a miracle. I do worry resentment will grow as she feels the pull of the yearning yet at the same time knowing she can't leave; wanting to go and not wanting to go…

We stay together but we both know the truth: She wants the sequel, but she can't underwrite the storyline, the actors, the director. I want the love and the safe place, but the cost is my self-esteem. I get to buy love because God knows I'm not worthy of any other kind.

As truth spills from my lips, I desperately try to think about something else—about new concepts using the word "immutable"—one is blockchain. This is a system of checks and balances that assures data added to the chain remains unchangeable. Interesting that in this day and age such a concept would need to be created to protect data.

What about people? Oh, the blockchain is to keep people from editing the data—a failsafe measure. People and data—becoming more and more alike—immutable data and immutable people. But people are not data, they're human beings.

The word immutable is also used to describe gender—as in fixed at birth. Now the phrase "gender is immutable" becomes part of a certain point of view. The very first time I ever saw the word "immutable" was in a sentence with the words "gender" and "fixed."

We connect the word "immutable" with data, and we use it with human beings. Does that mean human beings can be treated like blockchains—resulting in Blockchain People—people who need to be locked into their gender as a fail-safe measure? What are we guarding against? Where's the threat?

I understand the need to keep data safe, to keep people from changing it. But I don't see why there needs to be any fail-safe measure for gender. Yes, I have skin in the game. So, I'm not objective. Apparently, none of these "guardians of gender" ever fell in love with someone and later found out they had a really big secret.

Yes, there was an omission, a big one. Neither of us wanted to fall in love. My hugger/dancer tried to push me away, but for the first time in my life I didn't run. I knew what I wanted, and I went after it.

Would I have hung around if he had told me on our first or second date he liked to dress in women's clothing? Good question. We'll never know the answer, but I like to think my curiosity would have been piqued enough by the suggestion of an alternative lifestyle, especially given my puritan upbringing and my rebellious nature, that me, the writer, would have been all in.

And here I am trying to change the subject—trying to change someone's mind—my own. See how easily I get off track—blockchains! Then thoughts about not being able to change take me to regret. Would I regret deciding not to marry her?

How can I make decisions when I'm worried about whether I'll regret them? Is it that I don't want to be wrong—make the wrong choice? Or is a big part of it the fact I rarely make decisions for myself—I just let things happen—come what may. How easy it is to slip back to the way I've always done things. It works, so I repeat the pattern, never wondering whether my decisions are based on faulty information.

When I'm perfect, I have nothing to regret. Why can't I stop the pattern? I can't change because regret has a cost I don't want to pay. I will give up choice rather than have regrets. With perfection, there are no choices—I only see one path. Giving up choice has a cost for me. When I give up choice, I give up my voice.

As a writer, my sense of curiosity is stimulated by just a very small amount of information about something unknown, like pink lace panties. That lack of knowledge about soft and silky things triggers the need to learn more. The more I uncover, the more I want, and next thing I know I'm hooked. Pursuing a habit like curiosity can lead directly to the reward pathway in the brain.

Now I'm a gambler looking for the jackpot, an addict looking for a drug. I want more, to learn more. Sometimes fear stops me or at least warns me. But this time my fascination and newly discovered passion won out.

Here my ambiguous mind becomes an asset and I'm able to overlook my ignorance and fear because in a broad sense I'm learning and I'm writing.

Then she says, "Thank you for loving me." No one had ever thanked me for loving them. It was something new for me. Maybe it takes a certain kind of vulnerability to utter those words, an openness that comes along with feminine clothes and a sense of wonder—amazement that the glass I thought was half empty is in fact full. My response is always, "I do love you, very much. You make it easy for me to love you. I feel safe with you and your love."

Before I can even get the words out—

"But we need to talk about…"

Sal says, "I'm going to stop drinking." What? How did he know what I was going to say? Ah, it must have been my tone of voice, maybe my resolve, a new and different inflection.

"The drinking is no longer working for me," he confides.

Then I chime in, "Maybe we can get some help, a treatment center."

In a confident voice Sal says, "I can do it myself. I don't need help. I'm going to need to have something to do every day at three o'clock, like kayaking or fishing—something active that keeps me engaged." I'm skeptical, but I'm all about support and encouragement and so we begin.

Truth be told, we no longer take a cooler with us everywhere we go. I'm not sure where that cooler got to, but it could be the one he uses to prop up the lumber for his homemade weight bench. There are, of course, no more cigarettes. They were thrown away when the sprinting began—the start of a whole new healthy lifestyle. Not one to do anything in moderation, he goes on to be certified as a scuba instructor. Now that's what you get when you decide to ask for what you want, or at least start to ask with a new voice.

He tells me he loves me every day. I respond in kind. Sure, it's rote but it's a nice thing to hear. The sadness has been replaced by a resignation—to aging, comfort, routine. We have our cocoon, and we avoid reality. We live in a place where we're safe and we love each other. This above all is what we both want. Why would we change any of this? For something over there, just out of reach?

"How about living life to the fullest and routine be damned," says my hugger/dancer as his fingers reach out to caress my shoulder.

My pulse is accelerating just writing about our love and my heart is just beginning that achy feeling I get when I start to think about these things: my love for her and how long I've wanted to feel safe.

At first, I thought I could be detached enough to write and walk away. I've done it all my life. Now I'm not the one leaving. The pull of the road, the yearning, and the paradise just over the horizon become more than she can bear. In the distance, I hear Lee Marvin humming "Wand'rin' Star."

She holds me one last time, my hugger/dancer, and tells me she'll be fine once she gets on down the highway. I know I can't keep her here any longer, but my arms don't want to let her go. My body refuses to listen and the tears start to fall. I can't stop them, don't even want to. As she turns away, she touches my hair once more and says, "I'll miss you. I'll love you forever."

An imperfect pair, a paper bag love? Maybe, but I don't need to hold on to anyone who desires to be somewhere else. The trauma I've been dragging along in my paper bags all these years is born of a need to be attached because emotional bonding in my childhood was so elusive. Now my choice for a lover is someone unavailable, keeping me always trying harder to hold on. And so, I let her go.

Love is a curious thing. It can start with just a spark of intrigue about soft and silky things. When you add an investigative nature and an immutable object, the result is combustion. This is where paper bags come in handy—they're portable, temporary, and practical. I've even seen them used as kindling.

So, it turns out, lace panties are capable of moving an immutable object. With vulnerability, openness, and a sense of adventure, I found the love I was searching for. Mixed in with the satin and lace was something I finally recognized—the gift of love—the wonder of loving myself.

EPILOGUE

Sal is gone, but I never stop watching for her truck to pull into the campground. Tonight, I'm strolling through the RV park with Immutability and Regret, my daily companions. Even with all my self-knowledge—the yoga, healing, meditation—I can't seem to change. I'm still stuck on right and wrong, what would people think, boy pants and girl pants.

Suddenly, I hear all this clinking and clanging near the seawall. The sound, while unusual, is both disturbing and oddly comforting. I turn to see where the noise is coming from and I'm stunned by what I see: a giant in the blazing sunshine, holding something metallic that glimmers, something familiar—it looks like horseshoes—they're playing horseshoes.

Standing on a mound of dirt, they look seven feet tall. I'm pulled into their orbit; the talisman is a glimpse of home. In my mind I see my dad pitching horseshoes in our backyard. His only refuge from the kids and all the chaos. The sound of metal striking metal brings me back to reality.

Now I'm curious. Who is this horseshoe thrower? What are they doing here? The setting is mystical with the sun dropping over the horizon, the gleaming metal, and the oh-so-familiar sound. I'm magnetized and my body is being drawn toward them, as if I have no will of my own.

I feel my heart start to speed up. What's happening to me? I try to turn my head away from the blinding sun. I look over my shoulder for someone or something to distract me, but there's no one here. I'm alone and they're coming forward and reaching out to me. But the blazing sun, the flash of green, all I can see are spots. There is a scent however, familiar and musky. Impossible. It can't be. Moving as if in a stupor, I put my hand forward in greeting and they say,

"Kat, it's me—don't you recognize me? It's me, it's Sal."

I fall to my knees and reach up to touch a cheek, to brush the tears streaking across those beautiful hollows. Squinting, I try to stop my eyes from joining in the stream. Nothing can stop what is happening here—not my practical self and especially not my hands clutching my purse. I let go of the strings.

"What should I call you?" I blurt out, my practical mind recovering.

"I'm known as Sally, but *My Darling Sal* is my preference."

My mind is racing: Your place or mine? Clothes, no clothes? Talk first? Wedding? Commitment? Prenup? Legal? Call Eddie?

Breathe, just breathe...

The questions are meaningless. There is only one answer.

Sal kneels beside me, wipes her tear-stained cheeks, and sighs, "Thank you for loving me forever."

The seawall, where I first saw Sal emerge from the ocean, is only steps away. I can still remember the curly hair, the bronze skin dripping with salt water, the hand reflexively moving up to cover the grin, and those dimples.

"Hiya, I'm Sal, short for Salvataore."

I don't know Italian, but in Latin the word "savior" is at the root of Sal's name. "One who rescues from peril." If I hadn't met Sal, I would have continued in my perfectionist ways, never authentic, always fearful, following every rule, and never telling the truth.

Something extraordinary occurred under the awning of Sal's RV that night—a stunning revelation for the woman clad in iron panties. When I looked around for the textbook, the answer sheet, the catechism, I was adrift. I knew what my heart wanted but it was clearly wrong. So, I ran away in a monsoon with a dog no one wanted to shelter.

It seems kind of silly now. Why would anyone care what kind of fabrics Sal wears? That was a long time ago. What remains, however, are wisps of smoke, residue from the journals I burned in a panic when the immutable souls clamored for a return to yesterday.

In my mind, I can still hear that lilting voice encouraging me to be brave. I breathe a sigh of relief, and softly say, "Yes my dearest, a story has been told, a love is known, a secret has been set free."

About the Author

Trish McDonald, according to her DNA profile, is 86% Irish. For a storyteller, this "blarney" heritage comes in handy when writing about issues of childhood trauma. With a background in nutrition education, McDonald combines fiction and self-help in powerful scenes using science-based methods of body work: a yoga class, cranial sacral therapy session, reiki, music, and dancing. It is, however, the healing power of love and intimacy where her protagonist's journey leads to self-discovery and acceptance. An education writer, McDonald's credits include national publications, Family Circle President's Award for nutrition programs, and various academic journal articles. An avid camper, McDonald lives in a RV park in Southwest Florida. *Paper Bags* is her first novel.

For a discussion guide on *Paper Bags* visit the book page on woodhallpress.com. Visit Trish at http://www.trishmcdonald.com

Acknowledgments

I'm grateful to When Words Count Retreat: Steve Eisner, CEO, Peg Moran, editor extraordinaire, Amber Griffith, chef and all-around encourager.

To my beta readers: Maria, Judy, Stephanie, Nancy, Roberta, Mary, Catalina, and John —my heart is full.

To my sister Peg, for her support and encouragement—I love you.

To my 'Everyday' — you are loved.

To my readers: Thank you for buying my novel.